AMBUSH

"White Apache, listen!" Amarillo said. "More horses come!"

Clay spun. Sure enough, hooves drummed farther down the arroyo. "Against the wall!" he commanded, thumbing back the hammer on his rifle. Each of them cocked his weapon, and they were ready when more shadows came to a halt almost at their very feet and a rough voice bellowed, "Lookee! There's Lester's horse!"

"Forget the damn horse! Look down there! It's Lester himself!"

Inhaling, Clay leaped into the open, pivoting as he did, and shouted, "Now!"

Three scalp hunters were above. Three men all of the same stripe. Grimy, grungy killers who satisfied their lust for blood by slaying a people they rated lower than human. In their estimation the only good Indian was a dead Indian, and they had made scores of good Indians in their time. But their time ended then and there....

The *White Apache* series published by Leisure
Books:
#1: HANGMAN'S KNOT

2

WHITE APACHE

WARPATH

Jake McMasters

LEISURE BOOKS　　NEW YORK CITY

To Judy, Joshua, and Shane

A LEISURE BOOK®

February 1994

Published by

Dorchester Publishing Co., Inc.
276 Fifth Avenue
New York, NY 10001

Printed in the United States of America.

Chapter One

A rare cool wind blew out of the northwest, bringing welcome relief to the hot Arizona night. It whipped across the Mojave Desert, past the Harcuvar Mountains, then across the Sonoran Desert to the basin in which Tucson flourished and beyond.

Southeast of Tucson the breeze fanned Clay Taggart's brow as he squatted in high grass within a hundred yards of a frame house belonging to a rancher named Prost. But Clay hardly noticed. All he could think of was Prost, a man he had sworn to kill.

The prospect of making wolf meat of the rancher was so sweet it brought a grim smile to Clay Taggart's thin lips. He gave each of the twin ivory-handled Colts at his waist a pat, then firmed his grip on his Winchester and stalked forward, his blue eyes agleam with bloodlust.

Somewhere to the south a coyote yipped. Clay paid no heed. His thoughts were solely on his vengeance. For weeks now the only thing that had mattered to him was paying the twelve bastards back for the nightmare he had endured. His craving was like a blazing flame that seared the core of his being, preventing him from sleeping soundly at night and rendering him uncommonly restless during the day.

"I'm coming for you, you mangy polecat!" Clay whispered and stopped short, appalled at his lapse. He glanced to the right and the left, but the others were too far off to have heard, except for Delgadito, who was making a beeline for the stable and gave no sign of having noticed.

Relieved, Clay pressed on. His knee-high moccasins made little sound as he set down each foot. Even so, he was like a blundering bull in comparison to the stealth exercised by his companions. They were virtual ghosts. He knew where they were, could even see three of them quite clearly in the moonlight, yet not once did he hear them make the slightest noise. Small wonder their people were widely regarded as the scourges of the Southwest.

Clay closed his mind to such thoughts and concentrated on the front door of the house. There was only the one way in and out, so the others would be able to keep Prost from escaping if, by some fluke, the rancher got past him. The only real cause for concern lay in the three hands asleep in the bunk house. If they were loyal to the brand—and most cowboys were almost fanatical in their devotion to those they rode for—they'd pose a problem if they were accidentally awakened. Clay wasn't too worried though. Fiero, Amarillo, and Ponce were more than a match for any three cowhands.

When Clay was within a dozen feet of the house, he stopped. Delgadito and Cuchillo Negro converged on him and waited for his hand signal to advance and squat on either side of the door. Clay tested the latch, found it unlocked, and slipped inside.

The living room smelled like tobacco smoke. Clay was also sure he detected the lingering scent of whiskey in the air, but he told himself that was impossible; his senses couldn't be so sharp. Keeping low, he crept across the room to a narrow hall.

Loud snoring guided Clay to the bedroom. The door hung ajar. He pushed gingerly with his left hand, flinching as if struck when one of the hinges creaked lightly. The man on the bed sputtered, turned onto his side, and resumed snoring with gusto.

Clay rose into a crouch and drew his bowie knife. The keen blade glinted dully as he applied it to the soft flesh at the base of the sleeper's throat and growled in the man's ear, "Rise and shine, Prost! It's time to die!"

The rancher's eyes snapped wide, and he opened his mouth as if to shriek. But one look into the hard face above him and the feel of cold steel against his skin choked his outcry. He blinked and said, "Taggart? It can't be! You're dead!"

"You wish I were, you bastard!" Clay hissed. "The next time you hold a necktie social, you'd better be damn sure the rope does its job before you ride off and leave the guest of honor." His smile broadened. " 'Course, there won't be no next time for you. I'm the last innocent man you'll ever hang."

Prost gulped, then licked his lips. He went to sit up, but the bowie dug a bit deeper into his neck, freezing him in place. Mustering his courage, he said gruffly, "Now listen here, Taggart. You can't hold what happened against me."

"Like hell I can't!" Clay snapped, flushing with anger as he remembered the harrowing ordeal. "I'm going to make each and every one of you sons of bitches pay, and pay dearly."

"But we were a posse!" Prost protested. "We had to do as Marshal Crane wanted!"

Clay barely restrained himself from punching Prost senseless. "Since when does a posse have the right to hang a man without a trial? That's called a lynching, remember? And it's as illegal as sin." He shook his head. "You should have known better than to listen to Crane. When lawmen step outside the boundary of the law, they're no better than the lawbreakers they hunt down."

"I didn't want to hang you!"

"I didn't hear you object."

"What good would it have done? Crane wouldn't have listened to me." Drops of perspiration had formed on the rancher's forehead and upper lip. "There was no reasoning with him or those gunsharks who backed him up, Santee and Quarn. If I'd spoken up, they might have turned on me."

Clay touched the barrel of his Winchester to the scar on his throat. "So you let them do this because you're cold footed?" he said with contempt. "I ought to cut out your innards and strangle you with your own guts."

"Please! Let's talk this over. I'm certain we can come to some sort of agreement."

"Oh?" Clay lowered the bowie a few inches and drew back a step. "What sort of agreement?" he asked sarcastically.

The rancher slowly sat up. He looked at the closed window, gauging whether his hired hands would hear if he yelled for help. Then he stared at the bowie and decided not to invite instant death. It wasn't until that moment that he happened to notice the way Taggart was dressed. "My God! Look at you!"

Clay said nothing.

"You're wearing a headband, a breechcloth, and moccasins, just like some stinking redskin. Why?"

"Let's just say I've made some new friends since you saw me last and let it go at that."

Prost's forehead knit. Suddenly his mouth dropped open, and he jabbed a finger at Clay's bronzed chest. "You're the one the Army is looking for! The one they call the White Apache!"

This was news to Clay, unwelcome news that confirmed his worst fears. "The Army has posted circulars on me?" he asked.

"Not yet. But the last time I delivered beef to Fort Bowie, I heard talk about a patrol that tangled with a band of savages. They nearly got themselves wiped out." Prost paused. "One of the savages was supposed to be a white man, but I didn't really believe it could be true until just this minute. Riding with Apaches is as low as a man can go."

"Not if he owes them. Not if those Apaches saved him from a lynching."

"They what?" Prost exclaimed, astonished. "I never heard of such a thing! Why'd they save your hide?"

"I'm not here to chew the fat about them," Clay reminded the rancher. "I'm here to have you answer for my hanging, just like Jacoby answered for it."

"Art?" Prost said. "But he was killed by a rotten pack of renegades—" Prost stopped, gulped, and said, in horror, "Oh, my God! That was you!"

"He was the first," Clay admitted, a tone of regret in his voice. "I thought he was my friend. We used to buck the tiger together, drink together. Yet at my lynching he didn't say a word. All he did was check the knot on the rope so I'd swing good and proper." Clay snorted. "Some pard he turned out to be."

Prost listened attentively, or pretended to. While sitting up, he had been secretly working his right hand around behind him and under his pillow. Now his fingertips brushed the revolver he always slept with, and he suppressed a smirk. "Look, I agree we did you wrong," he said, stalling in the hope his unwanted visitor would look away for the fraction of a second it would take to bring the pistol into play. "I'd like to make amends, if you'd let me."

"How?"

"By going with you to the U.S. marshal and telling him everything. He has the authority to arrest a town marshal like Crane."

"You must figure I'm the biggest yack this side of the Pecos," Clay responded. "I'd be thrown into irons for Jacoby's death before I could get two words in edgewise."

"No one knows you were to blame. And I'd never tell."

"You expect me to trust you?"

"Suit yourself," Prost said with an exaggerated shrug that disguised the movement of his arm as he placed his hand onto the butt of his six-shooter. "I'm just trying to make good for my part in the hanging."

Clay Taggart thought for a moment. He gave the bowie a deft flip, grabbing the blade instead of the hilt, and began to lower the knife to his side. "Maybe you're right," he said softly. "Maybe I should tell all I know about Crane and Gillett to the U.S. marshal." Pivoting on a heel, he turned toward the doorway.

That was the moment Prost had been waiting for. Although a stocky man, he was exceptionally quick, as he proved by jerking his six-gun from under his pillow and leveling it in the blink of an eye. But as quick as he was, the man now known as the White Apache was faster. Prost's thumb was just curling the hammer back when Clay Taggart whirled, his right arm a blur. Too late Prost realized Taggart had thrown the bowie knife with practiced skill. Too late Prost tried to throw himself to one side, out of harm's way. Prost felt an intense, searing pain in his chest and fell back against the headboard. He gaped in growing shock at the hilt jutting from him and uttered a pathetic whine as rampant weakness assailed him. "No!" he said.

"Did you really reckon you could pull one over on me?"

Prost glanced up, saw Taggart's icy smile of triumph, and tried one more time to cock his pistol. To his dismay, Taggart took a swift stride and plucked the Remington from his hand as easily as if taking candy from an infant.

"Two down, ten to go," the White Apache said.

Tears welled up in Prost's eyes, and his lips moved soundlessly a few times before he blubbered, "Please—" Sluggishly lifting a hand, grunting from the exertion, he snatched at Taggart. "Please!"

"You'll get no mercy from me," Clay said, swatting the arm aside. "Not after what you did." He gingerly touched the scar again. "Not any of you. Not now. Not ever."

"Lord, no!" Prost rasped, his body sagging against his will, sinking flat on the bed where he gasped like a fish out of water and clutched feebly at the bowie. "I don't want to die!"

"And you think I did?" Clay retorted. "Miles Gillett used you, used all of you, and none of you had the grit to stand up to him." He bowed his head and balled his right hand into a tight fist. "I've never paid much attention to the Bible thumpers, so I have no right to be swearing by the Good Book, but I do swear that one day I'll make Gillett beg me for mercy just like you're doing. And when he does, I'll laugh in his face just before I slit him open from ear to ear."

Rage gripped Clay, rage so overwhelming he shook from head to toe, the same rage he had nurtured since the lynching, stoking it with the memory of the event as a man stoked a fire with logs, hour after hour, day after day. There wasn't the slightest shred of compassion in his soul for the men who had wronged him.

Once, Clay Taggart had been a rancher like Prost. Once, Clay Taggart had been a decent man who did his best to abide by the law and keep out of trouble. Once, but not now. He had a new creed that he lived by, a creed as old as the hills, a creed that he would follow until the day he died: An eye for an eye, a tooth for a tooth. He would do to others as they had done to him, and he didn't care a lick about the consequences.

"Damn you all to hell!" Clay said bitterly, and looked up to find his words had been wasted.

Prost was dead.

With a sharp wrench Clay yanked the bowie out, wiped it clean on the rancher's nightshirt, and slipped it into its beaded sheath. Grabbing Prost's revolver, he wedged it under the top of his breechcloth and turned to depart but halted in mid-stride on seeing a dark shape framed in the doorway. "Delgadito?" he asked in his heavily accented Apache.

"Lickoyee-shis-inday," said the stout warrior who entered and cast an indifferent gaze at the corpse. To Delgadito the only good white-eye was a dead white-eye, so the death of the rancher meant no more to him than would the passing of a horse or a mule. Indeed, the latter would effect him more since horse and mule flesh was a main staple of his people, and there was never enough meat to go around.

"You took a long time," Delgadito said, using small words so he would be understood. "I came to see if you were hurt."

"Thank you, partner," Clay said, resting a hand on the warrior's muscular shoulder. "I'm fine. Let's skedaddle while our luck holds out." He clapped the Apache on the back and headed from the room.

His features inscrutable, Delgadito trailed along. Inwardly, he was amused. He knew that Taggart mistook his concern for genuine friendship, a mistake the white-eye had made many times since they first met. Yet his interest in keeping Clay alive had nothing to do with liking the man, and everything to do with his plan to regain a position of leadership among his tribe. Taggart was a means to an end for him, nothing more.

Delgadito wondered how Clay would react if he were aware that Delgadito had been watching the whole time, ready to intervene if Clay needed help? Delgadito rarely let the white-eye out of his sight, but never revealed as much. A shrewd judge of character, the warrior was smart enough to know that keeping quiet was wiser, given Clay's temperament.

What a strange man, this white-eye! Delgadito marveled. So full of hatred for those who had wronged him, yet so unwilling to kill them outright with a single stroke or gunshot while they slept. Twice now, Delgadito had seen Taggart rub out his enemies, and each time Taggart had seemed more intent on talking them to death than on stabbing or shooting them.

Endlessly spouting empty words was the one trait all whites appeared to have in common. They reminded Delgadito of chipmunks with their constant chatter. It never failed to amaze him that such weaklings had been able to defeat his once proud people and drive the *Shis-Inday* onto the Chiricahua Reservation.

Delgadito stopped abruptly. Clay had veered to one side and was taking rifles off of pegs that were imbedded in the wall.

"Here. Take a couple," Clay said in English.

"We need bullets too," Delgadito answered in the same language, slurring the alien words. Since the first step in overthrowing enemies was understanding them, he had been working hard to master the outlandish tongue. Seldom did a day go by when he didn't find out something new about the strange *Americanos*. More importantly, he was learning their various weaknesses, weaknesses he would one day exploit to liberate the *Shis-Inday*.

Nothing mattered more to Delgadito than throwing off the bitter yoke of the arrogant whites. Every time he visited the reservation, every time he saw his people groveling for the paltry scraps of food and cheap clothing handed out in the name of the Great Chief in Was-i-tona, he could barely restrain himself from grabbing a weapon and running amok among the soldiers and reservation workers.

Who could have foreseen such a horrible fate for the once mighty Apaches? Reduced to the status of slaves! Delgadito thought, and then he had second thoughts. No, not slaves, not in the sense the whites had once enslaved the blacks. More like animals. Delgadito had heard whites speak of his people as inferior to their own kind. "Little better than dogs," one trooper had put it. Well, the white-eyes would do well to remember that sometimes dogs bit the hands that fed them, and if provoked, might attack their masters.

Delgadito turned as Taggart stepped to a cabinet in a corner and rummaged inside. Three boxes of ammunition were found for the two Winchesters and the shotgun Delgadito held.

"This looks like all there is," Clay said, holding the boxes in the crook of his arm as he hurried to the front door.

Outside Cuchillo Negro waited. The name meant black knife, a name he had earned when he slew a *Nakai-yes* in hand-to-hand combat with the man's own knife, a finely crafted blade sporting a large black hilt. He was never without his prized trophy, and he knew how to wield it skillfully, so skillfully he was rated as the best knife fighter in the Chiricahua tribe. Now he looked at Clay, saw the ammunition, and grunted in approval. "We go?" he whispered.

"The horses," Clay reminded him.

Cuchillo Negro was always the most cautious member of the band, the one least willing to take needless risks. This was certainly not out of cowardice, since he had proven his bravery too many times to have it questioned. Rather, he realized that because the Apaches were few and the white-eyes many, every warrior lost was irreplaceable.

Then, too, was the fact that Apache men were reared from childhood to honor two principle virtues: stealing without being caught and killing without being slain. The loss of a brave on a raid was a calamity to be avoided at all costs.

So, to reassure his reluctant ally, Clay whispered in his tongue, "It will not take long."

The three of them padded toward the stable. Clay saw Fiero crouched behind a bush near the bunkhouse and hoped the rash firebrand wouldn't do anything foolhardy. The warrior hated all whites, including Clay. It was safe to say that hatred was Fiero's ruling passion, and wedded to his fiery disposition, it made for an explosive combination. Clay never knew when Fiero might jeopardize them all by some thoughtless deed.

The stable door was ajar to admit air. Clay slid though the gap, paused so his eyes could adjust to the gloom, and moved down the central aisle checking the stalls. To his delight there was a horse in every one.

Delgadito and Cuchillo Negro knew exactly what to do. Speaking softly to the animals to soothe them into complying, the seasoned Apaches led horse after horse to the entrance. Ponce and Amarillo had appeared out of nowhere to slip ropes over the neck of each one.

Clay set down the ammunition and lent a hand. On a support beam hung several lariats which he appropriated. None of the horses resisted, none nickered or otherwise raised a ruckus. When the last animal had been given over to Ponce, Clay went to retrieve the boxes.

Ammo in hand, Clay hesitated, staring at the closed rear door. There might be more stock out back, he reasoned, in the corral. A quick look showed that all the Apaches had left. Should he go with them or take the time to see?

A sense of obligation took Clay to the rear door. He was obliged to Delgadito, and he always paid his debts. The Apache had spared Clay's life, had protected him from the others, had shown time and again the best of intentions. The least Clay could do was help feed the starving Apaches on the reservation with some fresh horse meat.

A pungent odor hit Clay as he swung the door wide, an odor he was all too familiar with from his years spent ranching, the odor of cow droppings and urine and sweat produced when cattle were penned in a confined space too long.

Clay was surprised to find the corral packed with cows which normally would be out on the open range at that time of year. He took several steps, searching for a horse among them, and was surprised again when the whole passel surged to its feet. "What the hell?" he said, amused the cows were so jumpy.

Not spying any horses, Clay was about to retrace his steps when he noticed there was something peculiar about the cows. They were much taller and leaner than the cattle he was accustomed to seeing.

Curious, Clay walked up to the nearest animal to study it. The cow backed off and gave a sharp snort. From the back of the corral came an answering bellow.

"I won't hurt you, you dumb critter," Clay muttered. He reached out to place a hand on the cow's forehead but it retreated until it bumped into other cows.

"You must be cactus boomers Prost found out in the chaparral," Clay speculated. The shape of the cows lent support to his hunch. They were shaggy and rangy, most with swaybacks and unusually exaggerated shoulder humps. The spread of their horns was equally remarkable, some boasting five or six feet or more.

Clay was so intrigued that he forgot all about why he was there and moved among them to try to identify the breed. A faint memory was jarred but he couldn't quite place it. "You're not polled Anguses, that's for sure," he said to himself.

Another bellow from the back of the corral made Clay turn in that direction. He glimpsed a huge form trying to press through the packed cattle toward him. A big steer, Clay figured, or maybe a bull, perhaps disposed to contest his presence. He decided to back out and go about his business, but when he pivoted to do so, he found his way was blocked by milling cows.

Clay gave one of the cows a stinging slap to get it to move, but it did no more than glance at him in annoyance. At that moment he recognized them for what they were, and a tingle of apprehension shot down his spine. He had blundered, blundered badly, and unless he got out of there quickly, he might well wind up dead.

Chapter Two

Arizona ranchers and farmers were rough, hardy souls. They had to be in order to survive. Not only did they have to fight roving bands of renegade Apaches and bandits, but they also had to fight nature. Blistering heat, fierce storms, and arid soil conspired to thwart them at every turn. Yet despite these hardships, the rugged men and women who called Arizona home managed to thrive. How? By being tougher than their adversaries, more ingenuous than the elements.

Irrigation enabled them to water the parched land; dams, to counter the constant threat of drought. They learned early on to breed livestock especially suited to Arizona's climate, and they were always on the lookout for ways to improve their stock.

So, when the ranchers heard about a vigorous new breed of cattle favored by the cowmen of west Texas, a few were interested enough to buy some for their own spreads. The rest waited to see whether the new breed would live up to its reputation and be able to adapt to Arizona's harsh conditions before spending any of their hard earned money.

Longhorns, the new breed was called. They were reputed to be able to flourish in any kind of brush country, even under the very driest of conditions. Steers four to eight years old averaged a whopping eight hundred pounds, the stories went, while ten-year-olds routinely weighed over a thousand. So much beef on the hoof—it was hard to believe.

But there were drawbacks. Longhorns tended to be temperamental and the wilder ones would attack a rider without warning. The older steers and the bulls were the worst, but the young steers and the cows would readily gore a horse or a man if riled.

For the most part, longhorns were allowed to roam the open prairie and were rounded up once or twice a year to be shipped to market. They didn't take well to being penned, and if cooped up long became extremely dangerous.

All these facts whisked through Clay Taggart's mind after he realized he was trapped among longhorns with an irate steer making its way toward him. He wanted to kick himself for being so careless. But he'd been unaware that Prost had invested in longhorns, and even if he had known, the last place he would have expected the animals to be was in the corral.

Clay girded his nerves and gave the cow blocking his path a firm shove on the flanks. The longhorn ponderously swung its big head, the tip of one horn nearly brushing Clay's shoulder. He shoved again, and this time the cow ambled off.

Yet another bellow reminded Clay of the brute trying to head him off. A glance showed the monster was ten feet away and closing in rapidly. The spread of its horns was tremendous, at least seven, possibly eight, feet. An old steer, Clay guessed, on the prod, eager to gore him.

Clay squeezed between the hind ends of two cows, then tried to go around a third that kept shifting position and barring Clay's passage. He opened his mouth to shout but changed his mind. A yell would rouse the hands, and he didn't want them killed if it could be avoided. His quarrel had been with Prost, not them.

The steer was only eight feet from him. Snorting and shoving, the monster forced the cows and younger steers aside with little difficulty.

Clay had to act, and act fast. He couldn't reach the sanctuary of the stable before the steer reached him, so he did the only thing he could think of: he hunkered down, squatting among a forest of knobby legs, hoping the steer would amble off if it couldn't see him. The cow smell was overpowering, which worked in his favor since the smell would hide his own scent. Or so he prayed.

Tense moments ensued. Clay stayed still, listening to the old steer snort. There was a commotion on the other side of the cow to his right. Tilting his head, Clay spotted the great dark muzzle of the steer inches above the cow's back and saw its nostrils flare as it tested the stale air.

Goose bumps erupted all over Clay's skin. He was tempted to bolt for the doorway but had no intention of committing suicide. Scarcely breathing, he began to edge around the hind quarters of the cow on his left.

The steer vented a rumbling sound, reminiscent of a stew pot about to boil over, and pushed against the cow in front of it. The cow, in turn, pushed sideways against Clay, nearly knocking him over. Clay had to throw up both arms to brace himself against the two cows, and when he did, the boxes of ammunition fell to the ground with a thud.

Suddenly the steer shoved harder and the cow tripped. Her large bulk swayed, looming above Clay's upturned face. She was going to fall on top of him!

Clay threw himself forward in a rolling dive that brought him to his feet a yard past the cow's flanks. In doing so, he exposed himself to the steer which immediately rammed into the tottering cow in an effort to get at him and sent the cow crashing down. Surrounding longhorns scattered, or tried to in the cramped confines, and in the next second there was noisy bedlam as the bawling cows and younger steers jostled one another while dashing every which way.

Caught in the middle of the bovine melee was Clay Taggart. Pounding hoofs tried to crush his feet. Heavy bodies smacked into him. He dodged the lethal tapered tip of a wicked horn and made for the high wooden fence, instead of the stable. Most of the longhorns ignored him. But not the massive steer, which plowed through the crowded animals as if through a field of grama grass.

Clay could feel the steer's hot breath on his back when desperation goaded him into a loco act. Using his right arm as a fulcrum to lever himself on top of the cow in front of him, he leaped, and for a fleeting instant, he crouched on her narrow back. Then, uncoiling, he leaped onto the back of the next longhorn, and leaped again, and again, jumping from cow to steer to cow, as if jumping across stepping-stones in a creek, each leap bringing him nearer to the fence. Behind him the incensed patriarch of the herd barreled past lesser animals.

Clay held the Winchester in both hands, using it to retain his balance as a tightrope walker would use a long pole. Only two cows separated him from his goal when his foot slipped, and he toppled forward. He would have plummeted between the cows had he not jammed the rifle's stock onto the last longhorn and allowed his momentum to vault him up and over.

The top rail rushed up to meet him. Clay alighted, trying to check his speed but couldn't. With his arms extended he dropped, striking the earth on his left shoulder. In his ears a resounding crash thundered as wooden rails splintered like kindling. Something struck him on the side, and he was sent tumbling to the left. More wood shattered. Hoofs drummed wildly.

The longhorns were stampeding. Thanks to the old steer, an avenue of escape presented itself, and they were quick to avail themselves of the opportunity. Bawling and kicking, they busted through the corral and raced out across the pasture raising puffs of dust in their wake.

Clay Taggart lay dazed close to an undamaged portion of the fence and watched them flee. Miraculously, none of the flying hoofs had trampled him. The old steer was at the head of the herd. It had forgotten all about Clay in the race to gain its freedom.

The night was abruptly shattered by war whoops and gunfire. Clay shoved erect and sprinted to the front corner of the stable. The shooting could only mean one thing. He wanted to prevent the Apaches from slaying the hired hands, but he was too late. Three bodies littered the vicinity of the small bunkhouse. One still moved, feebly. Fiero was bent over him, and as Clay laid eyes on them, the warrior lifted the cowboy's head by the hair and cut the man's throat with a single deft slice.

"The white dogs are dead!" Fiero yipped, waving his bloody blade overhead.

Ponce and Amarillo joined in. Cuchillo Negro stood

quietly next to a tree a score of yards away, six horses under his care.

Clay advanced, anger eclipsing his better judgment. He was fixing to give Fiero a piece of his mind when a hand fell lightly on his shoulder. Whirling, he discovered Delgadito.

"It could not be helped," the warrior said in Apache.

"I wanted to spare them if I could," Clay explained in English.

"I know."

Clay saw the warrior frown and assumed Delgadito was bothered that he was upset. Putting a hand on the Apache's arm, Clay said, "Do not worry. We are still friends."

Delgadito offered no reply. In truth, he was upset, but not because the white-eye was offended. Delgadito was upset because once again Taggart had behaved foolishly. What else had Taggart expected Fiero and the others to do when the white men came charging out of their wood lodge with their weapons spitting lead and smoke? At times like this Delgadito wondered if he was making a mistake in keeping Clay Taggart alive. Then he thought of his plan to regain a position of leadership among the *Shis-Inday*, a plan that hinged on the white-eye's unwitting help, and his doubts evaporated.

"We go!" Delgadito announced with a wave of a brawny arm. The other warriors hastened to gather horses, and presently they were all trotting across a field to where they had left their own mounts hidden in a maze of thickets.

Clay was somber, dwelling on the deaths. Perhaps he should be thankful. The Apaches, contrary to popular belief, did not routinely scalp their fallen foes. After a big battle, the Apaches would take one or two scalps so they

could perform their scalp dance, but generally they did
not lift hair as often as the Comanches or the Sioux.

Naturally curious about the custom, Clay had asked
Delgadito about it during one of their many long talks.
As Clay recollected, scalp taking was more a religious
affair than an act of mutilation. Each warrior who took
part in the battle needed to burn a few hairs in order to
drive the ghosts of the slain away from the weapons that
had killed them and to make the battleground free from
disease and ghostly influence. Or some such nonsense.

Clay's zebra dun pricked up its ears at his approach.
Untying the reins, Clay vaulted onto the bare back of the
horse Indian style. Several of the warriors were herding
Prost's animals into a compact group. Delgadito assumed
the lead, and at a signal from him, the band started to
the southwest. Clay fell in behind the horses and laid
the Winchester across his thighs.

The cool feel of the metal barrel caused Clay to think
of the ammunition boxes he had dropped, and he reined
up. In all the excitement of the stampede and the shooting
he'd plumb forgotten about them.

Clay went to give a shout, to let Delgadito know he
was going back for the ammo. But he didn't. He was a
grown man, not a yearling. He didn't need someone to
keep track of his comings and goings.

The ranch yard was deathly quiet, the house shrouded
in shadows created by the clouds that were obscuring
the moon. Clay rode past the dead cowboys, past the
front of the stable, and halted by the broken fence.
Dismounting, he let the reins dangle and strode briskly
into the corral.

Scores of drumming hoofs had reduced the boxes to
bits and pieces. The bullets were scattered over a wide
area, every last one covered with a layer of fine dust.

Some had been trod partway into the earth.

Kneeling, Clay commenced gathering the shells into small piles. Ammunition was too precious to be wasted. He must collect as much as he could before rejoining the Apaches. For minutes he labored, oblivious to all else until the metallic click of a gun hammer being cocked brought him around in a flash.

"Try it, you bastard, and I'll ventilate you good and proper!"

The speaker was a young cowhand, a thin man of eighteen or so, wearing worn jeans and a grimy white undershirt. He leaned on the fence with one hand while holding an old Dragoon pistol in the other, the pistol fixed squarely on Clay Taggart's torso.

"There's no need to shoot," Clay said softly.

"I knew it!" the cowhand exclaimed. "I knew you was white by the looks of you! Your face. Your build!"

"Yes, partner, I am," Clay admitted.

"Don't be callin' me your pard, you damned turncoat!" The man stiffened and held the Dragoon out further. "I heard about you from Mr. Prost. The White Apache, they've branded you. The murderin' devil who's gone over to the savages."

"It's not what you think."

"Like hell it ain't! I saw your red friends kill my *compadres!*"

"We figured there were only three of you. Leastwise, that's all we saw when we spied on the spread earlier."

"So you admit you're in cahoots with 'em," the cowboy declared spitefully. "You would of seen me if I wasn't so sickly. I've been airin' my paunch pretty near two days now."

"Sorry to hear it," Clay said. "I hate being sick, myself."

"Save your lousy pity! You sure won't git none when I turn you over to Marshal Crane in Tucson. Why, I expect the folks there will have you strung from the highest tree in no time."

Clay went to stand but the Dragoon centered on the middle of his forehead.

"Go ahead, give me an excuse."

"I'd rather talk this out if you'd oblige," Clay said, doing his best to remain calm. He didn't want to kill the younger man, if he could avoid doing so, but under no circumstances would he permit the cowhand to take him into Tucson. The last time he had been in Tom Crane's clutches, his life had been spared by a miracle. He couldn't count on his luck to hold a second time.

"Mister, I'll oblige you by pissin' on your grave. That's all," the cowboy responded. "Now git on your feet. And don't try no fancy moves. I don't much care whether I git you to Tucson alive or dead."

Clay could see the cowhand's face was slick with sweat. A single leap would bring him close enough to land a solid blow, but could he beat the man's trigger finger? Clay tried to stall by saying, "Can't help but notice your accent. Where you from? Alabama or Tennessee?"

"What the hell does it matter to you?" The man squinted an eye. "You wouldn't be tryin' to put a saddle on me, would you?"

"I'm not trying to buffalo you."

"Sure you're not," the cowboy snickered. "I've got news for you, four-flusher. Clem Bodeen don't fool so easy." Bodeen took several steps backward and waved the Dragoon. "Shuck all that hardware, pronto."

Reluctantly Clay obeyed, dropping the pistols and the knife. The Winchester was leaning against the fence near the puncher, who had not yet seen it. "What do you plan to do? Ride double with me?" he asked casually. "All your horses were taken."

"There's a few whey-bellies over to the west pasture," Bodeen replied. "They ain't much. But if I ride one and take an extra, they'll do to git me to Tucson."

"It's a long ride."

"I can hold up," Bodeen stated. "And if I don't, I can guarantee I'll put some pills into you before my lights go out. Now walk, you varmint."

Clay passed within a foot of the Winchester. It would have been so easy to lean down, scoop up the rifle, lever a round into the chamber, and fire. Easy, and fatal, with that big Dragoon aimed as steady as could be at his head.

"Lead your horse yourself," Bodeen directed. "Try forkin' leather and I'll shoot you in the back."

"The back?" Clay said as he clutched the reins.

"Any white man who would ride with stinkin' Apaches don't deserve no better."

Clay sighed and began hiking westward. "There was a time when I felt the same way you do. But things happen. People change."

"You'd never catch me stoopin' so low."

"Think so?" Clay said. "Let me tell you something, Clem. A man never knows how his life is going to turn out. Just when you think everything is grand as could be, life hauls off and wallops you one good. The next thing you know, you're up to your ears in more trouble than you ever wanted."

"You talkin' about yourself?"

"Could be. Could be you one day."

"Like hell. Nothing could make me do what you've done."

"Oh?" Clay glanced at the cowhand, who was off to the right. "Let's suppose you were in love with the finest women in all of Arizona. Let's suppose that one day her pa takes sick, and they can't afford to keep up the payments on their ranch. You want to help, but you don't have a lick of money. Then let's suppose that a neighbor, a rich rancher, comes along and offers to pay off all their debts if she will marry him. She doesn't want to, of course, but her pa is close to dying and she has her ma and three younger brothers to think of. And they all say she's a fool not to marry the rich rancher. So she up and does."

"What's all this got to do with anything?"

"Keep your britches on. I'm getting to that," Clay said. There was no need for him to justify his actions to anyone, but he wanted the young cowboy to understand, wanted Bodeen to know that he wasn't a blood crazed killer. "Now let's suppose this woman comes to regret what she did. She still loves you and wants to marry you and have your children. But the rich rancher isn't about to let her go. He's lusted after her since she was a girl, and he aims to keep her, no matter what."

"She should run off on the bastard," Bodeen said.

"It's not that simple. The rich rancher was true to his word and has been paying off her family's debts. Her pa recovered, but she's afraid if she goes away with the man she loves it might cause her pa's weak heart to give out. So she does the only thing she can. She slips away from time to time to see the *hombre* she really cares for."

"He ought to brace that rich bastard and fill him full of holes."

"Wouldn't work. The rich rancher never packs an iron. Everyone knows it. And he has the town marshal in his vest pocket. No, there's nothing for the man to do but keep seeing the woman on the sly and hope that somehow it all works out."

Clem Bodeen had lowered the Dragoon a few inches. "I think I'm beginnin' to follow your trail, mister. It doesn't work out for them, does it?"

Clay bowed his head, his voice lowering. "No, it doesn't. The rich rancher suspects something's up and has one of his hands, a hired gunshark by the name of Boorman, follow his wife when she goes off on one of her rides. Boorman finds her with the man she loves. There's gunplay. Boorman is a shade slower. The woman pleads with the man she loves to get away before her husband has the whole countryside out looking for him. Like a fool, he does as she wants."

"Why like a fool?"

"Because if I'd had any brains, I would have ridden to Gillett's spread and done him in then and there."

There was silence for a full minute.

"Jesus," Bodeen said. "Miles Gillett! You sure can pick your enemies."

"I try mighty hard," Clay joked, but neither of them laughed. "Gillett claimed that I was trying to force myself on Lilly when Boorman caught us. Claimed I shot Boorman in cold blood. Then Gillett sent Crane after me. And to make it all seem fair and legal, he had Crane deputize a bunch of local ranchers instead of using Gillett's gunnies."

"That Gillett doesn't miss a trick."

"He did this time," Clay said harshly. Stopping, he twisted and pointed to the scar on his neck. "They caught me, Clem. Caught me in the Dragoons and lynched me on the spot."

"Hellfire!"

"Then they rode off. Some of them were laughing."

Clay walked on, his words choked with emotion. "But they didn't know there were Apaches nearby. Didn't count on the Apaches cutting me down, saving my life."

"So that's why you hooked up with them!"

"Sort of. They agreed to help me get revenge on the sons of bitches who strung me up in exchange for me lending a hand against a scalp hunter who butchered their kin." Clay paused. "Prost was one of the men in that posse, Clem, one of the no-accounts who hanged me."

"I didn't know," the young cowhand said softly.

"Now you do."

This time the silence was much longer. Presently, Clem cleared his throat and said, "I ain't much for deep thinkin', mister—"

"Taggart. Clay Taggart."

"—and I don't have no right to judge you for what you've done. If the same thing had happened to me, I might have taken the same road. But that don't mean I can just let you ride off. Prost was one thing; my three pards, another. You had no call to kill them."

"The Apaches did it, not me."

"Doesn't make much difference, far as I can see. You're ridin' with them. That sort of makes you responsible for what they do, don't it?"

There it was. The awful truth staring Clay right in the face. "Yep," he answered in a whisper. "I reckon I am."

"Then I have to take you into Tucson. I'll tell folks how it was and maybe—"

Clay heard a strangled whine and spun to see Clem Bodeen sinking to the ground with an arrow jutting from between his shoulder blades. "No!" Clay cried, springing to the young man's side. Clem looked up, his eyes pleading, his mouth wide as if he was trying to scream but couldn't.

"As God is my witness, I didn't want this!" Clay said, holding the cowhand by the shoulders.

Bodeen trembled, gasped, and went limp.

Clay gently lowered the cowboy, then closed Clem's eyelids. He sensed, rather than heard, someone come up beside him, and he pivoted on a heel.

Delgadito had another shaft nocked on the sinew bowstring. A thin smile curled his mouth as he nodded at the puncher. "I come plenty quick when I find you gone. I save you, friend. You like, eh?"

Clay Taggart stared at the dead Southerner for the longest while. His reply, when it came, was as cold as ice. "If you only knew, friend." He pried the Dragoon from Clem's fingers. "If you only knew."

Chapter Three

Delgadito was troubled. He had expected Clay Taggart to be extremely grateful for being saved from the cowboy. Instead, the white-eye had been somber and surly all during the long journey back to the secret lair in the Chiricahua Mountains.

Warm Springs, it was called. There was only one way in and out, through a narrow cleft in a cliff. Only the Chiricahua Apaches knew of its existence; only they knew of the verdant valley hidden beyond the cleft and that a small army could hold out there for many months, if need be.

Clay had been to Warm Springs before. Oddly enough, he found himself anticipating their return with relish. The secluded refuge was the one place in the entire Southwest where he was safe, at least in one respect. The Army and the marshal couldn't lay a hand on him there. It was the only safe haven he had, the only place where he could take time to mull over his problems and ponder the best course of action. And he sorely needed to think things through. After what had happened to Clem Bodeen, he had to decide whether linking up with the Apaches had been a brilliant brainstorm or the biggest mistake he had made in a lifetime of making blunder after numskull blunder.

So, when the horses were let loose to roam and graze and the warriors gathered around the spring to talk in low tones, Clay went off by himself, scaling a lofty crag east of the spring to a wide shelf, where he perched and gazed out over the magnificent landscape.

Arizona had a stark quality that stirred Clay's soul. The sunbaked deserts, the lofty mountains, the vast canyons, and imposing buttes were all masterpieces of natural splendor. He never tired of admiring the scenery. Nor did he tire of the plant and animal life that so many Easterners found formidable. The cactus, chaparral, and mesquite. The Gila monsters, sidewinders, and scorpions. They were all part and parcel of a land that had forged living things on the unrelenting anvil of survival, rugged specimens capable of enduring the heat, the dryness, and anything else nature threw at them.

Once Clay thought he could hold up under any hardship, that he was tough enough to face any difficulty head-on and win out. But now he wasn't so self-confident.

What had he done of late to show he deserved a fine woman like Lilly? Clay thought. The answer: Not a damn thing. Everything had gone to hell in a hand basket, and he seemed helpless to prevent it from getting worse.

Lilly was still in Gillett's clutches. The law and the army were both on the lookout for him. Any white man in the territory would shoot him on sight. And to top it all off, he'd gotten involved with a pack of renegades, most of whom would as soon slit his throat as look at him. *What in tarnation had he been thinking of when he agreed to Delgadito's loco notion?*

Unknown to Clay, at that very moment, the subject of his thoughts was hunkered behind a boulder twenty feet away observing his every expression. Delgadito did not like the turn of events. He did not like the white-eye being so upset. If Taggart should change his mind about their arrangement, it would ruin Delgadito's well-laid scheme. And Delgadito was not about to let that happen. The Apache crawled to another boulder, crouched, and worked himself into a deep crack that shortly brought him to a vantage point a few yards above the shelf on which Taggart sat.

Delgadito could not permit the white-eye to dwell on whatever was bothering him. He had to keep Taggart too busy to even entertain the thought of striking off on his own. Consequently, Delgadito rose and descended along a rock incline to the shelf. He halted directly behind Taggart, then said in Apache, "We must talk, Lickoyee-shis-inday."

Clay was so startled, he nearly toppled off the edge. Turning, he glared in annoyance at the warrior and responded, "I would like to be alone."

"I will not take long," Delgadito said. He sat beside the white-eye and let his legs dangle. "This important." Delgadito looked up. "That right word? Important?"

"Yes," Clay said gruffly. "Your English gets better every day."

"Thank you," Delgadito said, beaming proudly.

"So what's so damn important?"

The tone of voice was an insult in itself. Had anyone else used it, Delgadito would have struck the offender

on the spot. He burned with resentment, but he kept his
temper and said, "You."

"Me?"

"You plenty upset."

"True. And I'd be obliged if you'd let me alone for
a spell. I have a heap to ponder."

"Tell me. I help."

Clay gave a little laugh and shook his head.

"You not want my help?" Delgadito asked.

"It's not that."

"What?"

Clay leaned forward, rested an elbow on his knee, and
cupped his chin in his hand. "Here I am, in the worst tight
spot of my life, heading for another Texas cakewalk if
I'm not careful, and the only one who gives a hoot is a
redskin most people consider the fiercest Apache in all
of Arizona." Clay chuckled. "This could only happen
to me."

Although Delgadito did not quite grasp the meaning
of many of the words Taggart had said, he did get the
general drift. "Why just you?" he asked.

"You'd have to know the story of my life to understand," Clay said wistfully. "My folks were nesters,
hardscrabble sorts who wandered all over the country
before pa settled near Tucson. That was a year to the
day before consumption claimed him. Ma wasted away
herself, after he was gone. They left me a homestead
that wasn't worth a hell of a lot, and I managed to turn
it into a small ranch. Made profits, too, my last three
years." Clay gnawed on his lower lip. "I miss that place
awful much."

"You want to go back?" Delgadito probed, suspecting
that here was the reason for Taggart's moodiness.

The idea hadn't occurred to Clay in many days, but

now that the warrior brought it up, he straightened and grinned. Yes, he most definitely would like to go, if for no other reason than to find out how his cattle were faring. Every last head had been out on the range when he left, so he figured they should all be fine. "There'd be no hard feelings if I were to light a shuck for home?" he asked.

"No."

"Good."

"We go with you."

Clay locked eyes with Delgadito. "There's no need."

"We help you find way out of mountains."

"I can find my own way easy enough, thanks. You've taught me well."

"We go anyway. Maybe other whites try kill you."

"I'll slip in and out before anyone knows I'm there."

"We go," the Apache insisted.

"It's too risky," Clay refused to back down. "My spread borders part of Gillett's on the north. He might have gunhands waiting for me."

"Then you need our help."

Exasperated, Clay averted his gaze so Delgadito wouldn't notice his anger. Truth to tell, he saw this as a golden opportunity to get rid of the Apaches once and for all. On his own he might be able to spirit Lilly away from Gillet. Together the two of them could head for parts unknown, California, maybe, or Montana Territory, anywhere they could start over and make a new life as husband and wife. "I'd much rather go alone," he grumbled.

Delgadito almost scowled in contempt at yet another example of the white-eye's weakness. *Americanos* had a tendency to feel sorry for themselves when things didn't go exactly as they wanted, to whine and complain over

every little hardship. An Apache would never behave so
childishly.

Yet, when *Americanos* were on the warpath, they
were worthy fighters who refused to retreat or surrender.
Delgadito had fought them, had marveled at their vigor
and fortitude. Small wonder the *Americanos* had defeated
the *Nakai-hey* many winters ago in a great war.

Delgadito could not understand, though, how a people
so like children on one hand could be so manly on the
other. *Americanos* were living contradictions, beyond
the ability of any Apache to fully comprehend. But their
contrary natures were predictable. They could be used
by one versed in *Na-tse-kes,* the Apache way of deep
thinking, which was so much more than thinking, more in
the order of a profound state of mind in which all factors
of a problem were considered and every contingency
allowed for.

Delgadito took a risk. If subsequent events did not
unfold as he anticipated they would, he stood to lose the
only chance he had of regaining a post of leadership. But
if they did, then he would have Clay Taggart at his beck
and call, a puppet like those the white women on the
reservation used to entertain the young ones, a puppet
to do with as he pleased.

"Very well, Lickoyee-shis-inday," Delgadito said. "It
will be as you want."

Clay glanced at the warrior in amazement. "You mean
it? You're not joshing me?"

Delgadito gestured at the horses grazing below. "We
cannot hold you here against your will, not after all you
have done for us. In the morning you can take your horse
and go."

Dumbfounded, Clay clapped the warrior on the back.
"Damn, partner, but you're more white than some whites

I know! I'll owe you for the rest of my days."

"If you decide to come back, you will be welcome."

"Thanks again," Clay said. He had, however, no desire whatsoever to return. Once Warm Springs was behind him, so were his days as the White Apache.

"I am happy to please you," Delgadito said, rising. "I will tell the others." Moving along the shelf to an incline, he started down the slope, listening to Taggart's whoops of delight. All four of his companions were regarding the *Americano* intently when Delgadito came to the spring.

"What is the matter with your pet?" Fiero inquired. "Has the dog finally lost his mind altogether?"

"I told him he could leave tomorrow," Delgadito said. The revelation had a chilly reception. As usual, Fiero voiced his sentiments first.

"He knows too much to be allowed to go."

"He knows nothing of importance."

Fiero motioned at the valley. "Is our refuge nothing? Are our secret trails nothing? The water holes known only to us, are they not important?"

"Lickoyee-shis-inday will not betray us."

"And that is another thing," Fiero said. "No white-eye deserves an Apache name. You have broken our custom and insulted our people by giving him one."

"There is a reason for everything I do."

"Was there a reason for letting our families be slaughtered by Blue Cap? Was there a reason for making us outcasts? Palacio and the rest of our tribe have not wanted anything to do with us since that scalp hunter took you by surprise."

"Soon we will be worthy again in their eyes."

"How?"

"You will see in the fullness of time."

"All I ever hear from you are words, words, words.

What have these raids with your white dog gotten us? How does he fit into your scheme?"

"My counsel is my own," Delgadito said stiffly. "You would do well to keep your own, unless you are eager to part with your tongue."

Tension gripped the group. Delgadito had thrown down a challenge, had told Fiero to mind his own affairs or else.

The other warriors fully expected their hot-tempered fellow to leap up and demand to settle the issue in personal combat. Cuchillo Negro put a hand on his knife, prepared to side with Delgadito if anyone else took up Fiero's cause. Ponce and Amarillo, however, showed no interest in doing so.

For Fiero's part, he was more puzzled than angry. None of this business with the white-eye made any sense to him, and he was at a total loss to explain Delgadito's recent actions. But of one fact he was certain. The wily Delgadito never did anything without cause. Among the Chiricahuas, Delgadito's faculty for *Na-tse-kes* was almost as legendary as that of the famed Mangas Colorado.

Fiero suspected Delgadito was somehow using the *Americano* to regain his lost standing in the tribe. But exactly how eluded Fiero. He wasn't a deep thinker, never claimed to be. He was a man of action and everyone knew it, a man afraid of nothing, happiest, in fact, when facing enemies in personal combat.

No, Fiero was not much of a thinker, so he did not know how to reclaim the general favor of his people, which he longed to do more than anything. While not outcasts in the strictest meaning of the word, Delgadito's band was shunned by the other Chiricahuas because Delgadito had seen fit to defy the tribal leaders and try to flee into the remote fastness of northern Mexico where Apaches had roamed wild and free from time immemorial. Secondly, and of crucial importance, Delgadito had failed and been cut off and tracked down by a large force of scalp hunters led by the despised Blue Cap, a demon who had taken more Apache scalps than all other whites combined.

Bad medicine, the other Chiricahuas said. Very bad medicine, and they wanted no part of it, no part of the warrior who had brought such calamity on the heads of those who had trusted his judgment and experience. And no part of the warriors who had joined his cause.

Fiero greatly wanted to change their opinion, to show them he had been right in siding with Delgadito, to prove his medicine was as strong as ever. He wanted to reclaim his rightful place as one of the most feared Chiricahua warriors, a man lesser warriors looked up to as courageous and invincible. To do that, Fiero had to rely on Delgadito's judgment, had to hope Delgadito's plan worked, had to keep Delgadito alive.

"Were anyone, other than you, to speak to me as you have done," Fiero now said, "his tongue would be on the end of my knife. But I respect your counsel. If you do not care to talk, I will not press you." Rising, he walked off.

"I never thought I would live to see Fiero back down to anyone," Ponce declared.

"He did not back down," Delgadito said.

"I just saw him," Ponce insisted. The youngest of the band, Ponce had not yet learned that the testimony of one's eyes was not always reliable.

"You saw him prove that he can think as fast as he kills, when he has to," Delgadito said. He walked away, grinning at the whispers that broke out by the spring.

They would learn. Eventually all of them would accept his wisdom without question. If, of course, Lickoyee-shis-inday did not disappoint him. And if he did, then Delgadito's knife would drink the white-eye's blood.

A pink glow painted the eastern sky when the White Apache rode out of the cleft and turned the zebra dun to the northeast. Clay kept glancing over his shoulder to see if the Apaches were chasing him. He couldn't get it into his head that they were really and truly letting him leave, not until an hour later when he crested a mesquite covered ridge, looked back, and saw no sign of pursuit.

"I'll be damned!" Clay exclaimed, and cackled for the sheer joy of hearing his own voice. "We did it," he told the dun. "We're shy of those pesky red devils once and for all!"

Clay applied his heels to the dun and covered the next mile at a gallop. A great weight had been lifted from his broad shoulders, and he felt so happy he could burst.

All the way to the San Pedro River, Clay thought about his precious Lilly, her lively green eyes, her raven tresses, and full figure. He couldn't wait to see her again, to hold her in his arms and smell the minty fragrance of her hair. Preoccupied as he was, he nearly made a fatal mistake.

Two days had gone by. It was the middle of the afternoon when Clay glimpsed the blue ribbon of the San Pedro ahead. He hadn't swallowed a drop since morning, and both he and the zebra dun were caked with sweat. Breaking the dun into a trot, he hastened toward a bend in the river.

A cluster of manzanita was all that separated Clay from the beckoning water when he heard low voices and the creak of leather. Instantly reining up, he slid off the dun, looped the reins to a branch, and moved warily through the manzanita until he obtained a clear view.

A Cavalry patrol had just finished watering their mounts and the troopers were climbing into their saddles. At the head of the patrol a captain sat astride a fine black and was observing. Once his men were mounted, he snapped his arm and barked, "Column, ho!" Swinging the black gelding, the captain rode straight for the manzanita.

Clay spun and raced to the dun, squirming between manzanitas that were closely pressed together, the limbs snatching at his face, cutting his cheeks. He burst free, grasped the reins, and led the horse to the south around the edge of the shrublike trees. He got the horse out of sight in the nick of time. The next moment the patrol swept past the manzanitas and headed out across open country.

Clay watched them leave, a hand over the dun's muzzle to keep it from nickering. The clatter and the thud of hoofs rapidly receded, and soon the patrol was no more than a cloud of dust in the distance.

Looking down at himself, Clay debated what to do. He had been inclined to go straight to Gillett's ranch first and seek out Lilly, so anxious was he to see her. But on second thought, he decided to change into his ranch duds before paying her a visit.

After letting the dun drink its full, Clay found a spot to lay low until sunset. He spent the time sleeping, resting up for the long ride ahead.

To reduce the chance of encountering whites with itchy trigger fingers, Clay had decided to travel at night until he reached his spread. Fording the San Pedro, he struck out to the northwest, relying on every trick Delgadito had taught him to avoid occasional travelers and, once, several heavily burdened wagons lumbering southward.

Clay was in familiar country again. He knew which roads were heavily used and which were not, and he chose the latter whenever he could. Cutting cross-country would have brought him to his ranch much sooner, but he stuck to the roads anyway. The cross-country route was the one an Apache would take, and he wasn't Apache.

Clay was among his own kind again and glad to be there. He would do things the way they did. The breechcloth, the moccasins, and the headband would all be burned, once he was home. He didn't want any reminders of his short stay among the savages.

An hour after sunset Clay heard a horse approaching from the northwest. He promptly angled into shrubs bordering the dusty road on the right and bent forward to blend his outline into that of the dun. In due course a lone rider appeared, a cowpuncher by the looks of him. The man was whistling softly, riding along without a care in the world. Clay waited, and when the whistling died, he went to resume his journey.

Hoofs sounded to the southwest. A pair of riders materialized, a man and a woman. The man was in uniform; the woman, a long dress and a bonnet.

The sight of the woman stoked Clay's hunger for Lilly. He stayed where he was, envying the young soldier, and heard their conversation as they slowly passed.

"—had a glorious time," the woman was saying. "We should go on a picnic again soon."

"The next time we won't go so darned far," the trooper replied. "It's not safe, I tell you, Vicky."

Light mirth peeled from the woman's lips. "Why, Lieutenant Darnforth, don't tell me you're afraid of a few measly redskins."

"You wouldn't take them so lightly if you'd seen the atrocities they've committed, like I have."

"Tell me."

"Never. It's not fit for a woman."

"Goodness, men can be too protective sometimes."

"Not where Apaches are concerned."

"What about the latest rumors? Do you think it's true, this White Apache story?"

"Must be. Headquarters sent dispatches to all the forts, advising us to make the capture of this man our first priority."

"I hope you get him, Don. Think how it would look on your record!"

"Whoever he is, I don't envy him. Every trooper in Arizona is on the lookout for his hide. If he's caught he'll be sent before a firing squad."

"You really think so?"

"That's the only fate such a traitor deserves."

"Ooohhhh. Imagine! I hope I get to see it. Wouldn't that be—"

Clay straightened as their voices faded. He stared at the road a moment, then wheeled the dun and headed cross-country. Mile after mile fell behind him. By the position of the stars and moon, the time was close to nine o'clock when he came to the top of a low hill and set eyes on the valley where his ranch was situated. Far off stood the buildings he knew so well, and he was shocked to see light glowing from the windows of his house.

Someone was there.

Someone who had no business being there.

Clay Taggart worked the Winchester's lever and galloped down into the valley.

Chapter Four

The frame house had been built in a cluster of trees fed by a large spring. Rafe Taggart, Clay's father, had found the site by accident. Rafe had been to see John Gillett, Miles's father, about buying a mule Gillett had for sale, but the mule had already been sold. On the way back to Tucson, Rafe had lost his way, drifting to the south. He'd spied a stand of trees and had gone there to rest in the shade. When his horse wandered off, he'd gone after it and found the animal drinking from the spring, which, at the time, was concealed by a large, dense thicket. In a country where water was more valued than gold, Rafe had done what countless others had dreamed about doing. Since no one owned the land, Rafe claimed it for himself and moved his family out the very next day.

Clay had many fond memories of the homestead and those eventful early years. He passed a certain tree as he approached the house and recalled the rope swing his father had made for him. Nearby was the stable in which he had spent many hours playing as a boy. His roots were here. This was the one parcel of land he loved more than any other. And it galled him that someone had seen fit to trespass, to make himself at home in his house.

A brown mare stood hitched at the rail. Clay halted beside the stable, slipped silently to the ground, and stepped to the corner. A shadow played briefly over the window in the front room, the glimpse too fleeting for him to note details.

Clay dashed to the west side of the house. The mare looked at him but, thankfully, did not act up. Once he had his back to the wall, he inched onto the porch, the Winchester clasped in both hands, a finger on the trigger. At the window he dropped to a knee and peeked over the sill. The curtains were parted a crack, and he could see the person bustling about within.

"Lilly!" Clay breathed, an electric ripple of joy shooting down his spine as he beheld the woman he loved carrying an armload of his clothes to the mahogany table. She had her lustrous hair up in a bun and wore a fetching blue dress sporting a big bow at the back.

Elated to find her there, Clay so forgot himself that he ran to the door, worked the latch, and threw it wide. Lilly whirled on hearing the sound, her features locking in a mask of total terror, her skin blanching. She dropped the clothes, pressed her hand to her mouth, and screamed.

"It's all right! It's me!" Clay cried, or tried to, for the woman he so adored swooned before he could get the words out. In two strides he was there, dropping the Winchester and catching her before she could strike the floor.

"Oh, dearest," Clay said fondly, drinking in her creamy complexion, the swell of her bodice. Her warm breath fluttered on his face as he carried her to the settee and tenderly deposited her.

Clay stroked her smooth forehead and couldn't resist pressing his lips to hers. She groaned, as if in the grip of a nightmare. Leaning the Winchester against the arm of the settee, he ran into the kitchen, grabbed an empty jar sitting on the counter, and went outside to the well his father had dug so the family would not have to drink from the same water as the stock.

It took but a minute to lower the bucket down and fill the jar. Then Clay sped back into the house, through the kitchen to the front room, and drew up in consternation on discovering Lilly had revived, taken his rifle, and was almost to the front door. At his entrance, she swung, bringing the Winchester to bear.

"Lilly, it's me! Clay!" he shouted.

Utter astonishment etched Lilly's lovely face. She recoiled as if she had been slapped but did not lower the rifle. "Clay? It can't be! You're dead! Miles told me that you were killed by Apaches!"

"Do I look dead to you?" Clay responded. He took a stride, stopping abruptly when the Winchester leveled at his midsection. "What's the matter with you? You should recognize me, even the way I'm dressed."

Lilly Gillett appeared on the verge of tears. She slowly let the rifle barrel fall and said, "It is you, isn't it? Oh, God! It is!"

Clay ran to her, embraced her, hugged her so hard she gave a little gasp. "Lord, how I've missed you," Clay said in her ear. "Many a night I lay awake thinking of you and dreaming of this day!"

For a while neither of them said a thing. Then Lilly pushed back and stared intently at him, studying him from head to toe. "I thought you were an Apache when you came through the door. Figured my time was up." She touched his cheek, his chin. "The sun has about burned you black. Where have you been? What really happened?"

"There's so much to tell I don't rightly know where to begin," Clay said, savoring the closeness of her, the scent of her skin.

"Start with after you shot Boorman, after you left me."

Clay guided her to the settee and set the rifle aside. She listened attentively as he told about his flight after slaying the hired gun, about the posse that showed up at his spread within the hour, about his flight to the southeast, to the Dragoon Mountains. "That's where they caught me and did this," he said, tilting his neck so the scar was conspicuous.

"You poor dear," Lilly said. "Yet you got away?"

In brief Clay related his rescue by the Apache band, the subsequent battle with the scalp hunters, and how he had fled deep into the Chiricahuas with Delgadito.

"So you've been with those red vermin all this time?" Lilly interrupted. "What have you been doing? How did you get away from them?"

"To answer your last question first, they just let me ride off." Clay paused, wondering if he dared reveal the rest. Lilly had a gentle disposition and might not approve.

"Were you their prisoner?"

"No."

"I don't understand."

"We had an agreement," Clay explained. "I offered to lend them a hand if they would lend me one."

"I still don't understand," Lilly said. "In what way?"

"Ben Johnson, the scalp hunter, killed their kin. I agreed to help them track Johnson down and, in return, they agreed to help me pay back the bastards who hanged me up to dry." Clay paused. "I never did go through with my end of the bargain."

"Pay back—?" Lilly said, her eyes widening. "That was you? You killed Jacoby and Prost?"

"You've heard about them?"

"Everyone has. The *Tombstone Epitaph* ran an account of the Prost raid just the other day. Every last hand was killed." Lilly shook her head in reproach. "How could you, Clay? How could you be party to such infernal butchery?"

Clay frowned. "You can ask me that after all we've been through? All *I've* been through."

"It's wrong, wrong as sin. I want your word that you won't kill anyone else until we've had a long talk."

"I didn't come all this way to flap my gums," Clay said angrily. "I came back to take you away. We can start over, Lilly. Move to Montana, where no one knows us, and build a ranch together. Or we can go to California, if you like. Miles will never find us."

"Oh, Clay."

"Say you'll go," Clay urged. "We can leave before midnight. I'll take you back so you can pack a small bag and slip out after Miles is asleep. By first light we should be halfway to the border."

"What a marvelous idea," Lilly said, covering his hand with hers, "but I can't leave so soon. Give me until tomorrow morning."

"Why? What difference does it make?"

"By the time I get home it will be very late. Miles will expect me to come straight to bed, so I'll have no time to pack. And if I sneak out of bed later, he might wake up. He's a very light sleeper. We can't afford to make him suspicious." Lilly squeezed his fingers. "I know how to get away without any fuss whatsoever. Early tomorrow morning Miles is going out to inspect some cattle, and after he leaves I'll pack and come right over."

"I hate waiting. I'd rather skedaddle while we still can."

"Trust me. My way is best."

Clay looked into her limpid eyes, and his resolve weakend. "I reckon one more night won't matter much," he said begrudgingly.

Lilly smiled. "I knew I could count on you." She pecked him on the lips, rose, and headed for the door. "Now I must be off. Already I've stayed too long. Miles might worry and send some of his gunmen to check up on me."

"Let them come!" Clay snarled, striding at her side.

"Control that temper of yours," Lilly cautioned, stopping in the doorway to lay a hand on his arm. "It's already caused us enough grief. Just dwell on tomorrow and how happy we'll be together."

"The two of us, together at last," Clay said. "It will be a dream come true." He raised her hand, kissed her palm. "I doubt I'll sleep a wink."

"Try, handsome. I don't want you falling asleep in the saddle." Lilly swiftly mounted the mare. "Take care."

"I should escort you to your doorstep."

"Be sensible. The punchers won't be asleep yet, and there are always gun sharks hanging around. I don't want them making wolf meat of you, not now when we're close to fulfilling both our wishes."

Clay didn't like having her leave by herself, but, he had to concede, she had a point. He waved until she blended into the night; then he jogged to the stable and swung onto the dun. Since she wouldn't let him take her home, he'd do the next best thing and trail her all the way back to insure she reached the Triangle G safely.

The moonlight made the task simple. Clay hung far enough back to prevent her from detecting him and maintained the same pace she did. When she slowed, he slowed. When she stopped, as she did twice for no apparent reason, he also stopped.

Approximately half an hour had gone by, and they had another fifteen minutes to go before they reached Gillett's sprawling house, when Clay heard the sound of riders approaching from the north at a full gallop. Fearing hostilities, he began to rush to Lilly's rescue, then drew rein when the night was rent by shouts in English.

"There she is!"

"Mrs. Gillett!"

"The boss was afeared for your safety, ma'am."

Further statements were too jumbled for Clay to make sense of. Simmering with resentment, he watched Gillett's men form a protective circle around Lilly and squire her into the darkness. Typical of Gillett, he mused somberly, to send men after her instead of going after her himself. The man never did anything he could have others do. Power and wealth did that to a person, made them too big for their britches. Miles Gillett was long overdue to be taken down a peg.

Swinging the dun around, Clay returned to his spread and bedded the horse in the stable. It took some doing as the dun balked initially at the strange enclosure, but once Clay had it snug in a stall heaped high with hay, the dun quieted and ate contentedly.

Clay went straight to the kitchen. His rumbling stomach demanded food, so he checked the pantry and cupboards and found all was in order. Someone, evidently Lilly, had been gathering the eggs his hens laid daily, and there was a basket of them on a pantry shelf.

In short order Clay had the stove lit and was frying a dozen eggs and chopped potatoes mixed with diced onions and shortening. He also made biscuits, smothered in butter. A bubbling pot of coffee completed his preparations. When he sat down to eat, his plate was piled so high he couldn't see the bottom. He chewed with relish, more cheerful than he had been in a coon's age.

Things were finally going his way, he thought. In twenty-four hours he would be on the trail with the woman who meant more to him than life itself. In two weeks they would be—where? Clay suddenly realized Lilly hadn't voiced a preference. No matter. They would be together. And in one year they would have their own place and be as snug and content as that horse in the stable. Their worries would be over. No more Miles Gillett, no more Marshal Tom Crane, no more Apaches.

The last thought bothered Clay. He should have been true to his word and gone with the band to wipe out Ben Johnson's vile gang. He owed them that much, at least. Delgadito had helped him when he'd needed help the most, had saved his life when any other Apache, and most whites, would have left him to rot under the blazing sun.

Taking a big bite out of a biscuit, Clay shook his head to derail his train of thought. No one could fault him for not keeping his word to a pack of redskins. Apaches were notoriously unreliable themselves, so he'd treated them no differently than they treated others.

But Clay kept seeing Delgadito in his mind's eye. Delgadito, who had persuaded Fiero and the others to conduct two raids on Clay's behalf. Delgadito, who had helped Clay get revenge and, yet, who had not objected when Clay reneged on his promise and rode out on them.

Clay had to admit he had done Delgadito wrong. But it was too late to cry over spilt milk. He had a new future to think of, the prettiest filly in the world to look after.

Once every last bit of egg and potato had been licked from the plate, Clay washed the meal down with four cups of steaming coffee. Feeling drowsy, he walked to his bedroom. As he entered, he glanced at the mirror above the chest of drawers and couldn't believe his eyes. Astounded, he gave himself a pinch. Was that him or an Apache?

Lilly had not been exaggerating. Clay's skin had been tanned a dark brown, so dark he might pass for a full-blooded Indian if not for his blue eyes. His hair, which hadn't been cropped in weeks, hung down, almost to his shoulders, the same length warriors wore theirs. Combined with the headband, breechcloth, and special knee-high moccasins, the effect was startling.

"This will never do," Clay said. He filled a basin with water, stripped naked, washed, and shaved using his straight razor, which was a welcome change from the knife he had used while living among the Apaches. The tangles in his hair took a while to get out with a comb. Next he took a pair of scissors to his head and gave himself a passable haircut.

Donning a pair of Levis and a shirt, he strolled barefoot to the kitchen and poured another cup of coffee. A closet in the hall contained an old pair of worn boots which he squeezed into with an effort. Upon going to the mirror again, he saw a new man, and he raised his cup in mock salute.

Packing took more time. Clay laid out his saddlebags and bedroll in the front room so they would be handy, come morning. He locked the doors, secured the windows, and turned in fully dressed.

Lying there in the dark, in the comfort of his own house, Clay felt a twinge of regret. He would much rather find a buyer for the ranch before leaving, but if he went into Tucson, Marshal Crane would throw him in the calaboose so fast his head would spin. Judge Abrams would preside over the trial, and everyone in Tucson knew Abrams and Gillett went back a long ways. A strangulation jig would be the end result. No, he'd have to forget about selling his property. As the old saying went, better to be safe than sorry.

Sleep was a long time coming. Clay was too excited at the prospect of living his new life with Lilly. He tossed and turned until the middle of the night and, at last, dozed off to have a fitful dream in which Miles Gillett, wearing an ancient suit of black armor and mounted on a black charger, attacked Lilly and him on the trail to Montana. The dream was perfectly ridiculous, as Clay concluded when he awoke at the crack of dawn to the crowing of his rooster out by the stable.

Clearing the bed in a single bound, Clay hastily washed up, making himself presentable. He wanted to impress Lilly with how he looked, to show her that he was the same man she had always loved and not some murderous turncoat who had gone Apache.

Clay didn't own a spare holster so he simply wedged the twin ivory-handled Colts under his belt, one on either side of the large buckle. He donned an old hat and gave his boots a quick shine.

A spring in his step, Clay hustled to the kitchen to make a new pot of coffee. He also made toast and finished off the last of the eggs.

The sun cleared the eastern horizon. Through the open kitchen window wafted scents Clay knew so well: the sweet odor of the dew-covered grama grass, the faint but unmistakable smell of cattle, and a hint of dust. Soon, though, the cool breeze gave way to the hot air of late morning, and Clay grew worried. Very worried.

Lilly should have been there by now, Clay told himself as he anxiously paced on the front porch. Something must have gone wrong. Maybe Gillett had caught her packing. Perhaps Gillett had changed his mind about inspecting cattle and stayed home. Or maybe there was another reason. Whatever, the morning waxed, and still Lilly didn't show.

Clay pondered whether to ride to the Triangle G or stay put. What if he was gone and Lilly came? Would she wait, or would she go on into Tucson, thinking something had happened to him? Indecisive, he kept pacing for another hour. Then he could wait no longer.

Since the dun was not accustomed to a saddle, Clay rode northward bareback. There had been a time when he'd looked down his nose at anyone, especially Indians, who rode in such fashion, but his time with the Apaches had changed his perspective. He actually liked riding bareback now, found it more comfortable.

There were several routes Lilly might have taken between the Triangle G and Clay's spread. He choose the likeliest, the shortest, and covered over five miles, always careful to stay near cover in case any riders appeared.

Two kinds of men worked for Gillett. There were ordinary cowhands who handled the cattle and other legitimate ranch work, and then there were the gun-hands, a dozen or so gun-wise leather slappers, whose only purpose was to safeguard Gillett and eliminate Gillett's enemies. Boorman had been one of the latter, with a reputation as one of the nastiest in a nasty bunch, and Clay entertained no regrets about killing the man.

Not long after Clay crossed onto the Triangle G, riders did appear. Clay was out in the open with nowhere to hide. His reaction was to lift the reins and to wheel the dun so he could flee to a knoll a quarter of a mile off. But he didn't. The riders, seven men in all, were traveling from east to west and would come nowhere near him. He had to remind himself that he was no longer dressed like an Apache. From a distance he would look like any other cowboy.

So, Clay brazenly rode on, waving when a couple of the riders did the same. The group never slowed and were presently out of sight. Clay chuckled, touched his heels to the dun to bring the horse to a trot, and covered another two miles without finding any sign that Lilly had passed that way earlier.

Frustrated, Clay stopped. He had gone far enough. Any further and he was bound to run into more punchers, who might take word to Gillett. Off to the northwest he spied cattle, a lot of them. Squinting he made them out to be longhorns. So Gillett had imported some, too.

Heading homeward, Clay laid out his plans for the rest of the day. He'd wait until nightfall, and if Lilly hadn't shown by then, he'd go after her. Thanks to the Apaches, he should be able to sneak right into Gillett's house undetected. He'd find Lilly, whisk her away, and be in Colorado within the week.

The burning sun created a haze that blurred far off objects. When Clay set eyes on his house and stable, they shimmered as if they were mirages. Drawing closer, he spied a horse at the hitching rail and a shimmering figure in front of the house, a figure with long black hair.

Clay whooped in delight and galloped forward. He removed his hat, waved it wildly, beaming like a kid who had just been given the greatest gift ever. Lilly

stood quietly, waiting with her hands clasped at her
slim waist, a grin touching her lips.

In a cloud of dust Clay reined up and leaped down.
"At last!" he bellowed, enfolding her in his arms. "I was
so scared you weren't coming!"

"It took longer than I counted on."

Clay shoved his hat on his head and took her dainty
hands in his. "Are you as glad as I am? I'm fit to bust,
I tell you! At long last we'll be together!"

"I'd never guess you were excited."

"You have no idea!" Clay laughed, then embraced her
again. He kissed her, or tried to, but she shifted and his
lips connected with her cheek. Belatedly he noticed she
was stiff, tense, and his pulse quickened as he stepped
back. "What's wrong?"

"I'm afraid I have some bad news."

"Bad news?" Clay repeated, his innards bunching into
a tight knot.

"We can't leave today."

"Why not?"

"For the same reason we can't leave tomorrow or any
other day."

"What?" Clay said, bewildered. "What the hell are
you talking about?"

"I'm not the one who should explain," Lilly said
sweetly. "He is." With that, she pointed at the house.

Clay looked and was transformed into a living block
of ice. For out into the open strode none other than
Miles Gillett.

Chapter Five

Overpowering rage coursed through Clay Taggart, rage so potent he shook from the intensity of it and flushed scarlet from neck to brow. He took a step, his hands poised to draw, and barked, "You! Here! Fill your hand, you son of a bitch!"

Miles Gillett had stopped at the edge of the porch and stood calmly, a mocking smirk on his face. "Everyone knows I don't pack an iron," he responded suavely, lifting the flaps of his expensive jacket to prove his point. "Kill me, Taggart, and you'll be wanted for two murders."

"Do you think I care?" Clay roared, beside himself with fury spawned by this man who had caused him so much misery, who had stolen Lilly from him. "You're buzzard bait!"

Oddly, Miles Gillet laughed. "I reckon not, you stupid bastard. Not unless you want Lilly caught in the cross fire." He held out a hand, then loudly snapped his fingers.

From around both sides of the house came gunmen. Others came from inside. Still more appeared at the stable. Eleven hard cases, their pistols drawn or rifles leveled.

Clay noted their cold, implacable expressions, and knew they would have no compunctions in cutting loose with Lilly so close to him. He motioned at her, whispered, "Move to one side, pronto, so I can draw on these polecats."

"I can't do that," Lilly said.

"Don't worry about me. Just run!"

"No!"

Exasperated, Clay twisted to give her a shove but froze when a six-shooter cracked, the lead smacking into the earth between his legs.

"Just be still, senor, and you will live a little longer."

The speaker was a sturdy Mexican wearing a wide-brimmed sombrero, a white shirt with frills, a brown jacket, and embroidered pants that flared out at the bottom and barely covered his huge spurs.

"Surgio!" Clay snapped.

"*Sí*, senor. We meet again."

Surgio Vasquez was one of the best trackers in the whole Southwest and a bad man of some note, who favored a nickel-plated Colt sporting seven notches. It was Vasquez who had tracked Clay down for the posse, Vasquez who had recaptured Clay, after Clay briefly escaped their clutches.

"I owe you," Clay growled.

"But what can you do with the senora right there, *tonto?*" Vasquez asked, sneering.

There was nothing Clay could do, and they all knew it. Clay glanced right, glanced left, then glared at the man he hated with an abiding passion. "I should have known you wouldn't fight me fair and square."

Gillett snorted in contempt. "Fight you fairly? Honestly, Taggart, sometimes you amaze me. You seem to think the whole blamed world should be as self-righteous as you are. This isn't a poker game we're playing. It's for much higher stakes than that, the highest a man can go after."

"A good woman," Clay said.

"What?" Gillett responded, his smirk back. "Oh. Yes. For lovely Lillian." Gillett laughed again strangely and pointed at Clay's midsection. "Lose the irons, and do it mighty carefully."

Shoulders slumping, Clay complied, the twin Colts thumping at his feet. As soon as he was disarmed, the gunnies converged, two taking him by the arms and propelling him toward the house. They wrenched him to a standstill shy of the porch. Another hard case knocked off his hat, then slapped his face.

"Now, now, boys," Miles Gillett said. "There will be plenty of time for that. For now I want to enjoy this. I want to see the look on his face when he learns the truth."

"What are you talking about?" Clay demanded.

Gillett hooked his thumbs in his belt and stepped down. Up close, he presented an imposing figure, as tall as Clay but twice as wide and not an ounce was fat. His slicked hair was brown with a trace of gray at the temples. His face was square in shape, his nose thick and broad at the bottom, his lips fleshy. A thick mustache partially hid his cruel mouth, a clipped beard framed his jutting chin. "The truth," he stated smugly.

"Which you wouldn't know if it jumped up and bit you on the ass."

Some of the hired killers chortled.

Gillett glanced past Clay and said, "Why don't we show the poor deluded fool, my dear? Seeing, after all, is believing."

An invisible knife sliced into Clay's abdomen and carved its way upward as he saw Lilly sashay past him and mold her voluptuous form to Miles Gillett. She kissed Miles, a lingering, loving kiss, their lips working as their tongues probed, and Clay felt the knife pierce his heart. A sour taste filled his mouth, and, for a moment, he thought he might be sick.

Lilly grinned when she broke for air. She draped a slender arm on Gillett's shoulder, winked at Clay, and said, "The best damn lover this side of the Mississippi."

Raucous laughter greeted her remark. Surgio Vasquez yipped and spun in a small circle.

"Do you understand yet, you pathetic simpleton?" Miles asked, his thick fingers idly stroking Lilly's hair. "Has the truth sunk in?"

Dazed, his body tingling as if numb, Clay answered softly, "She never loved me, did she?"

It was Lilly who responded. "I thought I did, once, when we were young. Miles showed me how wrong I was, showed me the difference between loving a boy and loving a man."

"But you came to me after you were married. You told me that you didn't care for him, that you wanted out so you could be with me," Clay said.

Gillett sighed. "Haven't you ever fished, Taggart?"

"Now and then."

"And how do you catch one? You bait the hook with

the kind of bait the fish you're after like best. Lilly was
my bait, the kind you couldn't resist."

"You sent her to me? You wanted to stir up my old
feelings for her?"

"Of course."

"Why?" Clay asked, a tremor in his voice.

"Haven't you figured it out yet?" Gillett released Lilly
and pivoted, nodding at the house, the stable, the well,
and the valley beyond. "The Bar T is small but you have
fine grassland here. And your spring can keep a large
herd watered."

"You did all this to get my ranch?"

"What else? I told you we were playing for the highest
stakes there are."

Clay sagged, his head spinning, and would have fallen
if not for the men holding him. So many shocking
revelations, one on the heels of the other, had drained
him of emotion and strength. He had been betrayed by
the woman he loved; she had used his affection to lead
him like a lamb to the slaughter. "Boorman," Clay said.
"He was part of it?"

Gillett nodded. "Only the jackass wasn't supposed to
go and get himself killed. The plan was for him to gun
you down; then Lilly and him were to claim he had to
do it to preserve her honor." The big man snickered.
"I reckon Boorman's rep as a gunfighter was a mite
overblown."

Clay closed his eyes and wished they would shoot
him to put him out of his misery.

"I figured you'd catch on after the posse showed up
here so soon after the shooting," Gillett went on. "There
hadn't been time for anyone to ride to Tucson and tell
Crane and for Crane to round up the men he needed."

"He did show up quick," Clay said, wondering why

he hadn't realized it sooner. How blind he had been! A bigger jackass than Boorman. The biggest jackass ever.

"Because I thought ahead," Gillett bragged. "A wise man covers every angle, so I wanted Crane ready to go after you in case you got away. I had him deputize other ranchers so folks hereabouts wouldn't suspect it was all my doing."

"I knew that much," Clay said feebly.

"Did you? Did you also know I arranged to have you lynched?"

Clay's eyes snapped wide. "You couldn't have. Some of them are men I've known for years."

"But only casually. You're a hard man to get to know, Taggart, keeping to yourself all the time like you do. Yes, some of those men played poker with you on occasion, but they didn't consider you their pard. Take Jacoby, for instance. When I offered him a thousand dollars, he agreed to help hang you without a second thought. Hell, he even offered to tie the noose himself."

Jacoby had been the one who insisted on checking the knot before Clay was strung up. The galling memory rekindled the rage Clay had felt on first seeing Gillett. "And the others?"

"It varied. Heskett settled for seven hundred dollars. Denton only five hundred. Prost wanted some of my longhorns—"

"Those were yours?" Clay blurted.

"Longhorns cost top dollar. You don't think a small-time rancher like Prost had the money to buy any, do you?"

All the pieces were coming together, all the fragments forming into a horrifying whole. Clay had not only been deceived by the woman he'd longed to marry, he'd been betrayed by every man he had ever felt halfway close to, by men who'd known him since he was a youngster. Pards or not, they should have refused to help Gillett and warned him of Gillett's plot.

"Yes, sir," Gillett said. "I had it all planned out. Then those rotten redskins went and saved your worthless carcass."

"You know—?" Clay began.

"Lilly told me," Gillett divulged. "Told me everything you confided in her. Frankly, I thought you were stringing her on until she brought up that you never lie. And you were hanged." He stared at Clay's scar. "Damned if you don't have more luck than anyone I ever heard of."

"This *hombre's* luck has run out, Senor Gillett," Vasquez interjected.

"That it has," Gillett agreed, grinning. "You might say he's reached the end of his rope."

Clay listened to their mirth and bowed his head. Not from embarrassment or guilt over his stupidity, but to concentrate, to control the volcanic fury boiling within him. He gritted his teeth, clenched his fists, and bunched his muscles.

"Look at him!" someone said.

"Is he wetting his pants?" asked another.

Lilly Gillett twittered gaily.

Suddenly Clay exploded, flinging both arms outward. The two hard cases were caught off guard, sent staggering to either side. In a flash Clay took a half step and punched, ramming his knobby knuckles full into Miles Gillett's mouth. The rich rancher stumbled backward, his boot heels hit the porch, and he fell. Lilly started to scream, her cry cut off by the fist Clay slammed into her temple.

In a flurry of blows the gunhands pounced, bearing

Clay to the ground by their sheer numbers. There were too many of them, though, and in their haste to hit him they struck one another. Oaths and inarticulate yells mingled with the thud of blows.

Clay was pummeled without letup, but most of the punches glanced off him or caused little pain. Fueled by his rage, he lashed out again and again, gauging his swings with care, landing brutal hits on chins, knees, and noses. One gunman was knocked backward by a smash to the jaw. Another tottered off, clasping a bloody face.

Suddenly Clay set eyes on a Colt in a holster. He lunged, grabbed the butt, lunged again to the right while thumbing back the hammer, and fired as his shoulder smacked the ground. There was a screech and the gunmen began to scatter, some clawing for their pistols.

Clay snapped off another shot, rolled, and fired once more. He was rising to his knees and taking deliberate aim at Miles Gillett, determined to bring Gillett down before the hired killers brought him down, when a jarring impact to the side of his head caused the world to swirl and mist blackly. He tried to resist the mist, to overcome the pain, but a second blow pitched his body to the ground and his mind into an inky emptiness. The last sound he heard before the veil claimed him was the shrieking voice of his beloved Lilly.

"Kill him!" she was screaming. "Kill the bastard! Kill him! Kill him! Kill him!"

Clay seemed to be floating in a roiling pool of liquid pain. He didn't want to be there so he thrashed and kicked. Then a yellow glow blossomed above him, and he tried to reach it.

Unexpectedly, Clay revived, and immediately wished

he hadn't. He was on his back, his arms and legs bound, in what appeared to be a dark room. Agony lanced him from head to toe. His face was terribly sore, his mouth felt swollen. Trying to sit up only worsened the agony but he persevered and was almost upright when a door in front of him opened.

"I knew I heard something, Senor Gillett," Surgio Vasquez called out.

The light enabled Clay to recognize his own bedroom. Heavy footsteps heralded the arrival of a trio of hard cases who assisted Vasquez in carrying him down the hallway to the kitchen. He smelled food and his mouth watered.

Miles and Lilly Gillett were at the table, eating well-done beefsteak and potatoes. Miles glanced up, his eyes smoldering, and scowled. "So glad you could rejoin us, Taggart. I didn't think you'd recover after my boys got through stomping you into the dust." He paused. "You're one tough son of a bitch."

"Why didn't you shoot me and get this over with?" Clay asked testily.

"That would be too easy. After all the aggravation you've caused me, I want to do this properly." Miles set down his fork and touched his puffy lower lip. "You'll pay for this, a hundred times over."

"If bluster were gold you'd be the richest man in the country," Clay countered.

Gillett glowered, rose partway, then stopped and sat back down. "There you go again, getting the better of me when I should know enough to ignore every word you say. Why do I let you get under my skin the way I do?"

"Guilty conscience," Clay taunted.

"I don't have a conscience. Ask anyone." Gillett

folded his arms across his chest. "I want you to know how I've set this up, just so you'll feel worse."

"Go to hell."

"If hell exists, you'll get there long before I do." Gillett leaned back and grinned. "I aim to kill you the way an Apache would, slowly and with a lot of suffering. I reckon that's fitting since you've taken up with the red scum."

"You think they're scum? There isn't an Apache alive who can hold a candle to you."

"Really? I'm flattered." Gillett laughed. "Once you're dead, we'll bury you where no one will ever find the body. Then, in a week or so, I'm going into Tucson and have my lawyer arrange to buy your ranch from the person you named as beneficiary in your will."

Jolted, Clay struggled to a sitting position. "I don't have a will!"

"You do now," Gillett said. "Duly signed and witnessed." He chuckled. "Your signature is a forgery but it's good enough to fool anyone except an expert."

"And just who did I leave my ranch to?"

Lilly leaned toward Clay and arched her eyebrows. "Can't you guess? For over a year now Miles has had the men spreading stories all around about how you loved me so much you couldn't stay away from me. How you pestered me to divorce him and marry you. How you wouldn't take no for an answer."

"I think ahead," Gillett declared. "I didn't want any suspicions aroused when you were shot."

"You've wanted my ranch all that time?" Clay marveled.

"Longer," Gillett admitted. "My own range has been overstocked for far too long. In order to expand, I bought out all my neighbors who would sell. The only two who turned me down were you and that hermit, Jeb Wilson."

Clay remembered Old Jeb, as folks called him, a kindly gent who had owned several hundred acres east of the Triangle G. Jeb had been content to raise a few cows and poultry and live quietly in a small shack. A year and a half ago Jeb had disappeared; everyone had blamed the Apaches. "You had Jeb killed, didn't you?"

"Hell, I killed the old fart with my bare hands," Gillett revealed, "then filed on his land before his corpse was stiff. Since he had no will and no next of kin, it was easy as pie."

"So I'm the last holdout."

"Correction, Indian lover. You *were* the last holdout. The Bar T will become part of the Triangle G before the month is over." Gillett's mouth screwed upward. "I can't thank you enough for your generosity. I'm so obliged, I'm going to celebrate by making love to Lilly in your own bed."

"Oh, Miles!" Lilly said. "You're so naughty sometimes!"

Clay looked at her in rank disgust. Was this the same woman who had impressed him as being so kind, so decent? The woman who had gone on long rides with him and talked of nothing but the joy they would know together? The woman who had promised to be true to him until the end of time? The woman who had shared her body with him more often than he could count? Who had said such tender words when they were caressing one another? *Was this bitch the real Lilly?* "God, I've been such a fool," he breathed.

"That you have," Gillett said. "And you're long overdue to earn a fool's just reward." A hefty hand flicked at one of the gunmen. "You know what to do,

Jensen. Take Crist and Volk with you. And remember. I want to hear his screams."

"You will, boss," Jensen promised.

The night air was refreshing. Clay breathed deeply as he was hauled to the stable where Crist lit a lantern and hung it on a peg. Volk and Jensen dragged Clay to the middle of the aisle, under a thick beam. Rope was produced, and a minute later they had Clay hanging by his arms several feet off the ground.

"Fetch it," Jensen said to Crist.

Clay watched Crist leave. Volk whispered to Jensen, and they both glanced up at him and laughed. Whatever they had in mind was bound to be unbearably unpleasant, and he hoped he wouldn't give them the satisfaction of screaming like Gillett wanted.

Presently the man named Crist returned. He was skinny enough to get work as a scarecrow, with features to match. In his right hand he grasped a coiled bull whip.

"Get ready to lose some hide," Jensen told Clay. "Crist is a wizard with that blacksnake of his."

"Feel free to holler all you want," Volk added. "It'd make the boss mighty happy."

Clay glared at both of them. "I won't let out a peep," he vowed.

The whip uncoiled with a snap, the lash landing close to Clay's moccasins. Crist snickered and gave the handle a shake. "You'll holler all right, mister. By the time I'm done, they'll hear you clear in China." He cracked the whip again. "I can take the eye off a fly at twenty feet. Got my start years ago as a bullwhacker."

In anticipation of the ordeal to come, Clay clamped his teeth and forced his body to relax. *I can handle the pain,* he mentally assured himself, over and over.

Jensen leaned against a stall. "I don't reckon this *hombre* believes you're all that good, pard. Why don't you educate him?"

"I've been looking forward to this," Crist said. "Any bastard who would ride with Apaches deserves to have his skin peeled off, bit by bit." He nodded at Volk. "Strip off his shirt, so I can get to work."

Clay swayed when Volk grabbed hold. There was a ripping sound and his shirt was thrown down. The air felt cool on his skin, bringing to mind the distant Dragoons where high up in the Apache stronghold the air was always cool, always—

CRACK!

Exquisite anguish lanced Clay's back. Involuntarily, he arched his spine and gasped; his thoughts jumbled, his teeth clamped harder.

"I see you gritting your nutcrackers, Injun lover," Crist commented. "It won't help after a while. You'll be screaming whether you want to or not."

Clay opened his mouth to respond, which was a mistake. *CRACK!* The lash bit into him again, searing him with torment. He cried out, not loudly, but loud enough for the three hard cases to hear and laugh.

"Real tough, ain't he?" Volk said, to no one in particular.

"They all act tough at first," Crist said. "The black-snake loosens their tongues soon enough."

Even though Clay was braced for the next blow he had to bite his lower lip to keep from shrieking. It felt as if his back had been split down the middle and there was a moist sensation creeping down his spine.

"Want us to jam a stick in your mouth?" Crist poked fun at him. "Would that help?"

CRACK!

CRACK!
CRACK!

A flood tide of pain engulfed Clay, forcing a whirlpool of sickening impressions; his back was on fire, his mind reeled uncontrollably, and his stomach threatened to heave. He gulped, gritted his teeth, and stared at Crist, refusing to be beaten in spirit, as well as body.

"That's right. Show us what you think you're made of," Crist said, grinning. "But I've got bad news for you, Injun lover. I'm just getting warmed up. The worst is yet to come."

Clay saw the bullwhacker's arm move and closed his eyes. It didn't help. Crist was right. It only did get worse. And worse. And worse.

Chapter Six

The floor of the stable had miraculously changed into a great red sea. Through a scarlet haze Clay Taggart stared dumbly at the moist red liquid below him and idly wondered how the miracle had been accomplished. Then he observed a large crimson drop fall into the sea followed shortly by another and he believed that he knew the answer: It was raining red rain.

"He's come around again, Crist."

"Time to get back to work."

Clay heard the words but they held no meaning for him. They seemed oddly slurred—or was his hearing at fault?—and echoed from the bottom of a vast cavern. Something pricked his back, making him flinch, and vaguely he realized he was being whipped, for the sixth or seventh time. He hardly felt the strokes anymore. There was so much pain, so much acute, terrible pain, that a little more didn't matter to him at all.

More drops cascaded into the red sea. Clay could see

each drop clearly as it fell, see the ripples it made on contact. How pretty it was, he reflected. So pretty it brought a lump to his throat.

Clay's gaze strayed to the front entrance. He dimly recalled seeing two people there, a big man and a woman who had laughed at him, the woman doubled over and laughing louder. Who were they? What had they found so funny?

Suddenly others appeared at the entrance, three dark figures who hurtled out of the night with gleaming blades in their outstretched hands. They wore breechcloths and moccasins and their long black hair was bound by headbands. One of them pounced on Volk. Another, whose ugly face was aglow with fiery glee, attacked Jensen. The third, the most muscular of the trio, came straight for Crist and caught the bullwhacker from behind as Crist was raising the bullwhip to strike again. Three knives streaked in the lantern light; three gunhands fell. So swiftly was the deed done that none of the white men was able to yell.

Clay watched the muscular one stab Crist again and again. At last, the Indian rose and stepped up to him. Hands touched his shoulders. Then he was falling, slumping forward over the wide shoulders of the warrior. "Delgadito?" he said. "Is that you?"

"Quiet, Lickoyee-shis-inday. We must get you away from this place."

"Well, I'll be damned," Clay mumbled. He wanted to say more, but a black hand of fog plucked at his brain, and he drifted off. Once, he awoke to a rhythmic rising and falling motion and guessed he was draped over a horse. Another time, he came around when cold water was splashed on his face. The sky was brightening, and he heard horses neighing. He licked his lips, tried to talk, but dizziness whirled him into oblivion again.

* * *

Delgadito squatted close to a small fire and stared at the white-eye sleeping peacefully on the other side. Soon would come the crucial test. If he had judged Taggart's character rightly, then the next phase of his plan could be carried out. If he had misjudged, he would finish the job the white eyes in the huge wood lodge had started, and he would not be so sloppy about it. He fingered the hilt of his knife and waited, noting the breaks in the sleeping man's deep breathing.

Soon Clay Taggart groaned, then opened his eyes. Crackling flames were close to his head, and through them he glimpsed a squatting Apache whom he recognized right away. "Hello, Delgadito," he said in Apache.

"Hello," the warrior responded in English.

"Where am I?" Clay asked in that language as he tried to sit up. To his dismay, he was too weak to do so.

"Warm Springs."

"You brought me all the way here?" Clay twisted his head, saw the narrow valley with its high walls of stone. "How long have I been out?"

"Four sleeps since we bring you."

"Four days?" Shocked by the disclosure, Clay mustered enough energy to rise onto his elbows. "You've been taking care of me all that time?"

"Yes."

Clay was genuinely touched. No one else would have done such a considerate thing for him, certainly not Lilly or any other white person he knew. "I'm obliged for my life a second time," he remarked.

"You do for me, I do for you."

"Maybe so," Clay said, "but I'm still in your debt." He hitched at a blanket that had been draped over him.

"I'll always be in your debt." His shirt was gone but he still had on his Levis and boots. Bloodstains dotted the top of his pants, stains that recalled the severe whipping, and he reached behind him to gingerly probe his back. He didn't need to see to know his skin had been cut to ribbons and was badly swollen. But, to his astonishment, there was little pain. He mentioned as much.

"I use herbs," Delgadito said. "Take away hurt."

"You did a fine job. Teach me how to use those herbs someday."

Delgadito looked at the ground so the white-eye would not notice the secret delight he felt. "I will. But you go back once you better, no?"

Clay glanced at the Apache. He hadn't given any thought to what he would do next, so he said, "I honestly don't know what I'll do once I'm on my feet."

"No hurry," Delgadito said. Rising, he turned toward the spring. "I get you water, then get food. You must be plenty hungry."

"Starved enough to eat an antelope whole."

"You eat, drink, rest," Delgadito advised. He added, almost as an afterthought, "Soon we go hunt Blue Cap. You stay here, get better, when we are gone."

Blue Cap. Ben Johnson. Clay stared at the Apache's bronzed form as Delgadito walked off. The warrior hadn't said a word about Clay's former promise to help them get their revenge, yet Clay hadn't forgotten, and in light of his rescue by the band, he couldn't deny his obligation any longer.

Over at the spring, Delgadito picked up a gourd and dipped it in the cold water. Cuchillo Negro and Amarillo were seated nearby; Fiero and Ponce were hunting.

"Have you asked him?" Cuchillo Negro inquired.

"He will speak about it when he is ready," Delgadito responded, raising the full gourd out.

"Why do we need him along?" Amarillo wanted to know. "He will slow us down and get in our way."

"Would Fiero and Ponce go if I offered to lead us?" Delgadito brought up.

"No," Amarillo said. "They still do not trust your judgment after you let Blue Cap catch us unprepared at the hollow."

"But they will follow if Lickoyee-shis-inday leads?"

"They would not be content to stay behind and let a white-eye do that which they should do themselves," Amarillo said.

"Now you know why we need him," Delgadito declared. He carried the gourd to Taggart and took his place by the fire.

Clay sipped slowly. Several more gourds were scattered close to the blanket, gourds Delgadito must have used to feed him while he was bedridden. "About Blue Cap—" he said.

"Yes?"

"I'd like to tag along."

"This is our fight, not yours. You stay."

"I was there, remember? I saw Johnson's cutthroats butcher your women and children. I saw babies hacked to pieces, young girls and boys run down and crushed under the hoofs of horses. I saw his men lift the hair of Apaches who were still alive." Clay rested the gourd in his lap. "It was a massacre, the sort of slaughter Johnson is famous for. And I want to do my part to see that he never does it again."

Delgadito allowed himself the luxury of a smile. "If you want to come, Lickoyee-shis-inday, then come. You can lead us like last time."

"Me?" Clay had understood when Deladito requested he lead the raids against the men who had lynched him since he knew most of the ranchers involved and had visited their spreads once or twice. But this was another story. "I've never been to Mexico."

"Not matter. You lead. We help you find way."

"Your friends might not cotton to the notion."

"We do good when you lead. Take many horses, many guns. You are good medicine. They like you to lead us."

"Even Fiero?"

"Fiero always have pepper in blood."

The description was so accurate it made Clay chuckle. "Yep. I've known his kind before." He took another swallow. "Fair enough. I'll do as you want. And after we return I'm going to get my own revenge on Miles Gillett."

"Gillett?"

"The son of a bitch who framed me and is fixing to steal my land out from under me. I need time to think, to come up with a brainstorm to stop him. There has to be a way."

"This Gillett, one who have you whipped?"

"He's the one," Clay rasped. "In his own way, he's as bad as Blue Cap." Clay reached over his shoulder and pressed his palm to the lash marks. "I'll carry his brand for the rest of my days."

"And woman you wanted to see. Lilly?"

Clay's features clouded. "She's a viper too. She used her charms to pull the wool over my eyes. And when I was hanging from that beam like bloody meat, she laughed at me, Delgadito. Laughed until she was red in the face."

"You kill her too?"

"Kill Lilly?" Clay said, appalled by the suggestion. Killing a woman went against his grain. Despite Lilly's treachery, he couldn't bring himself to imagine his hands on her throat.

"She turn on you," Delgadito said. "She hurt you inside where hurt never heals. She should die like Gillett."

"I can't just rub her out," Clay protested.

"Why not?"

"She's a female, dang it."

"Female?"

"A woman. One of the fairer sex," Clay said.

"I know not all your words, White Apache. What does it matter? Apache women, Apache men, same. Apache woman harm Apache man, she die."

"I'd rather get even with her another way."

"As you wish," Delgadito said, adding yet another weakness to his growing list. Who ever heard of men so cowardly they could not put a wayward woman in her place? Inspiration struck, and he ventured to offer, "If White Apache wants, I will help him. I rub out Lilly for you."

Not knowing what else to say, Clay replied, "That's awful obliging. I'll let you know if I decide to take her life."

Delgadito grunted. Everything had turned out just as he wanted, and he was extremely pleased. He had the white-eye eating out of his hand, like a camp dog. "I go fix food," he announced.

"Wait," Clay said, sitting up. "There's one thing I'm a mite curious about." He glanced at Amarillo and Cuchillo Negro. "Don't think I'm not grateful for having my hide saved, but what the dickens were you doing at my place? Why'd you show up when you did?"

Delgadito had foreseen being asked that exact question and had readied an answer. "You say we welcome to come by for beef anytime for saving you from hanging."

"I did, didn't I?" Clay said, and grinned. He owed his life to an offer made on the spur of the moment with no real expectation of seeing the Apaches take him up on it. "Tell you what. Once Blue Cap is out of the way, I might be able to help you get your hands on more horses and beef than you've ever stolen at any one time."

"That fine," Delgadito said, then left.

Leaning back, Clay propped his head in his hands and gazed at the beautiful azure sky. Here he was, back among the Apaches. Any man with the brains of a turnip would be terrified to death and anxious to be elsewhere, yet strangely enough, he didn't feel the least bit afraid.

Clay ran a hand through his tousled hair. As he lowered his arm, he paused, studying his deep tan. He recollected Lilly's statement about his resembling an Apache so closely she hadn't been able to tell the difference, and he remembered the picture he presented in the mirror.

Was he turning Indian? Clay asked himself. Did that explain why he felt no fear at being among the renegades again? Was he really dumb enough to believe the Apaches could be trusted? That any one of them wouldn't slit his throat the moment it suited their fancy?

Sighing, Clay eased onto his side. He didn't consider himself an Apache, not by a long shot. Circumstances he had no control over were responsible for his being where he was. If he'd had his druthers, he'd be on his way to Montana with Lilly. But it wasn't meant to be.

Thinking of Lilly brought to mind her betrayal. Should

he have seen it coming? Should he have suspected she was leading him on? He'd automatically figured that since he loved her, she loved him. Life didn't work that way, though, did it?

Clay had to face facts. He had been played for a fool, had made a monumental jackass out of himself. Anger flared, and he thought of how rewarding it would be to get even with the Gilletts, to bring them to ruin as they had ruined him, to have them groveling at his feet, begging for mercy.

But how to go about it? Clay wondered. It was doubtful he could bring it about on his own. Miles Gillett was too powerful, too rich, and had too many gunmen working for him. Clay would need help. Special help.

Clay stared at the Apaches. They were all the special help he would need. Maybe, provided he played his cards right, he could use them to do the job. He still had to work it all out in his head, but there had to be a way to bring Gillett down.

Or was he going at the problem the wrong way? Clay reflected. Shouldn't he be more concerned about clearing his name than getting revenge? If he could prove Gillett had masterminded a plot to strip him of the Bar T, he could reclaim the ranch and either go on living there or sell out and move to a place where no one knew him, where no one would be laughing at him behind his back for being such a yack.

Clay shifted to relieve a cramp. Everything depended on what Miles Gillett did next. If Gillett went to the law and reported that he was alive and let it be known he was the so-called White Apache, he'd never be able to clear himself, never be able to show his face among white society again.

There were so many things to think about that Clay's

head swam. He wasn't a deep thinker, never had been. He had no idea which course of action was best. But he had to decide soon. As his father had often said, "Any man who makes it a habit to straddle the fence all the time always walks around with a sore crotch."

Fiero and Ponce appeared at the mouth of the canyon, a dead buck strapped to a limb carried between them. There was no denying the hostility in the glance Fiero shot in Clay's direction. Clay ignored the troublemaker and shut his eyes to catch some rest.

The next Clay knew, loud voices had woken him from a brief nap. The Apaches were arguing. Fiero was nose to nose with Delgadito and gesturing excitedly. Delgadito was his usual calm self. When Fiero stopped to take a breath, Delgadito responded in a low, level tone.

Clay had witnessed the same scene too many times to care one way or the other what the argument was about. Fiero was always causing trouble; the man had the disposition of a wildcat. A wildcat with a very short fuse.

Footsteps warned Clay someone was approaching. He glanced up and was surprised to find all five warriors bearing down on him. Propping himself on an elbow, he glanced around, seeking anything he could use as a weapon, just in case. There were only a few small rocks.

"Lickoyee-shis-inday!" Fiero barked. "I would speak with you."

Clay selected his words carefully and spoke Apache as clearly as he could. "What can I do for the man who helped save me from my enemies?"

"I was not there just to save you," Fiero responded. "I came because it was a chance to kill white-eyes, and I never pass up a chance to kill your kind."

"I still thank you."

Fiero placed his hands on his hips. "Keep your thanks. Delgadito wants you to lead our raid on Blue Cap. I do not think you have earned the right." He sneered defiantly. "What do you say to that?"

"How do the others feel?" Clay asked.

"We have all agreed except Fiero and Ponce," Cuchillo Negro answered for the rest.

Clay faced the firebrand. "Who do *you* want to lead the raid?"

"Anyone besides you," Fiero said.

"Then you do it," Clay said, and deliberately laid back down, cradling his head on his arm. A long silence ensued. He didn't need to look at Fiero to know he had embarrassed the warrior by making the suggestion. Fiero had long aspired to be a leader but his own temperament had stood in his way. None of the other Apaches cared to put their lives in the hands of a man known to be reckless and unpredictable.

"I cannot lead," Fiero said harshly.

Making a show of impatience, Clay sat back up and pointed at Ponce. "Pick him to do it."

"The youngest warrior is never the leader of a band," Fiero said. "It must be someone with experience."

"Have Cuchillo Negro or Amarillo be in charge."

"Neither of them wants to."

"Delgadito, then."

"He is responsible for the massacre. He cannot lead us again until he has reclaimed our trust."

"So who is left?" Clay asked, knowing full well the answer. "Me? But you do not want me to do it. So I guess there will be no raid, and your loved ones will not be avenged."

Fiero squirmed inwardly. Once again he had spoken

without thinking, and once again he had made a fool of himself. As much as he despised the fact, the white-eye was the only logical one. "You lead us," he abruptly declared. Wheeling, he stalked off to be by himself.

The crisis over, the Apaches dispersed. Delgadito and Cuchillo Negro walked toward the cleft, Delgadito scarcely able to hide a grin. He was proud of the way Lickoyee-shis-inday had handled the situation. To be truly great, an Apache had to do more than plunder his enemies without being caught and slay without being harmed, he had to be persuasive in councils. White Apache had proven he had such a rare gift by forcing Fiero to admit the truth, even though Fiero did not want to.

Delgadito looked over his shoulder at the white eye. He had to watch himself or before he knew it he would develop genuine affection for the man. Already he was thinking of Taggart as an Apache—a bad sign. Delgadito did not dare let himself become fond of the *Americano*, not when Delgadito might have to kill him later on.

"He did well, the one you have adopted," Cuchillo Negro commented unexpectedly.

"I do not recall adopting anyone," Delgadito said.

"White Apache might as well be your son, the way you treat him."

"I treat him no differently than I do any other white eye."

"Any other white-eye would have been long dead," Cuchillo Negro countered. "I do not know what it is about him, but you like him a lot."

"Have you been drinking *tizwin* or mescal and not told anyone?"

"I wish I had been," Cuchillo Negro said wistfully, "but there is none to be had and you know it." He caught sight of a hawk soaring high on the air currents and slowed. "You will not admit as much, but you do not regard White Apache as you do most whites."

"He is a means to an end, nothing more."

"Lie to the others if you must, but not to me. We have been friends for too long, Delgadito. I know you as well as I know myself."

"You think you do."

"I know you have it in your mind to kill him once he is no longer of any use to you. But when the time comes you will not do it."

"I will do what I must."

Cuchillo Negro's eyes sparkled. "Care to wager on that?"

The challenge stopped Delgadito. His people were known far and wide as ardent gamblers, willing to bet on anything and everything, and he was no exception. Many times he had lost practically all he owned on the roll of a hoop or the flip of a card. "What would you wager?" he asked.

"Five good horses."

"You bet high."

"And one rifle."

"Very high."

"I know I will win."

"Very well. I accept," Delgadito said. "But remember whose idea this was. I do not want you to complain when I hold your rifle in my hands while riding one of your fine horses."

Cuchillo Negro chuckled.

And over by the fire the subject of their conversation looked in their direction, smiled, and waved.

Chapter Seven

In Arizona, and elsewhere in the American Southwest, the Apaches were universally hated and if caught outside the reservations, killed on sight.

In Mexico the situation was much different. One state, Chihuahua, had made peace with the Apaches, going so far as to give bribes in the form of food, blankets, clothing and other items in exchange for being left alone. An Apache could wander into any town in Chihuahua without fear of being set upon and slain.

In the neighboring state of Sonora the exact opposite held sway. Apaches were ruthlessly exterminated, a practice encouraged by the Sonoran government which offered large bounties for Apache scalps. As a result, several roving bands of vicious scalp hunters roamed the arid Sonora countryside year-round, fattening their pokes at the expense of Apache lives.

And not always Apaches lives. Since the government officials overseeing the program had no way of telling a

Pima scalp from an Apache scalp, there were widespread
rumors the scalp hunters had slain many peace-loving
Indians, long friendly to the Mexicans, and claimed the
scalps as genuine Apache hair. Although the friendly
tribes protested, the state government made no effort to
investigate. Sonora wanted the Apaches exterminated at
any cost.

Into this slaughter ground came the White Apache
and five warriors in early summer, traveling on foot
due south from the Dragoons. They hugged the western
base of the Sierra Madres until they reached the Yaqui
River where they camped on a tableland that overlooked
a frequently used crossing. Northwest of them lay the
town of Hermosillo, where a garrison of *soldados* was
quartered.

Clay Taggart was once again dressed in a breechcloth,
moccasins, and headband. Across his chest were slung
two cartridge belts. On his right hip hung a long knife;
at his waist were two Colts. He held a Winchester in the
crook of his left arm as he surveyed the sluggish Yaqui
and inquired in English, "How long will we have to wait
before they come?"

"I do not know, but they *will* come," Delgadito said.

"How can you be so sure?"

"We will let them know we are here."

Clay didn't like the sound of that but he couldn't
object. Although they had picked him as their leader,
he didn't have the same influence a chief would. He
couldn't tell them what to do or what not to do. His main
purpose was to settle disputes, which mainly involved
keeping Fiero in line.

"We will show them why they will never beat us,"
Delgadito had gone on. "We will cause them such misery
they will cry out to Blue Cap for help."

That evening Clay learned what Delgadito meant. The band headed for Hermosillo, winding among the foothills until the lights of a rancho appeared. In single file, and as soundlessly as specters, the Apaches crept toward a cluster of adobe buildings from which gay music wafted. The casa was well lit and there appeared to be many people inside.

Some sort of celebration, Clay figured. He was at the rear of the line, strongly wishing he were somewhere else. He'd agreed to help the Apaches in their fight against the scalp hunters, not to slay innocent Mexicans. For two bits, he mused, he'd go back to the tableland and wait for them.

Then it became too late to do anything. A door opened on the east side of the house and out walked several laughing *vaqueros*. A couple of them must have drunk too much tequila because they swayed unsteadily as they made for a stable.

Delgadito promptly veered to intercept them and the other warriors imitated his example. In order to keep the Apaches in sight, Clay did the same. He hung back, though, so he wouldn't have to kill anyone.

The *vaqueros* were almost to the stable doors when the Apaches struck. Instead of slaying quietly, Delgadito and his fellows opened fire, blasting the *vaqueros* in a withering hail of lead. The gunfire and war whoops brought the music to a stop. There were shouts in the house, a door was flung wide, and a number of men rushed out to be met by a fusillade that dropped five or six in the grass and drove the rest indoors.

Clay spotted Fiero sneaking into the stable. Shortly thereafter smoke poured out the entrance, and soon flames were visible within. He glanced at the casa, expecting the occupants to charge out to put out the

flames and save the squealing horses, but there was no
movement and no sound, as if those in the house were
too scared to make a noise.

It was well known that the Mexican people held
Apaches in the utmost terror. Decades of Apache
depredations had instilled in them a sense of dread
bordering on awe. When Apaches were known to be in
a certain vicinity, country dwellers flocked to the nearest
town for protection. Mothers only had to threaten to leave
their unruly children outside for the Apaches to find to
get the children to behave. So it was no wonder there
was little resistance now.

Clay saw a figure appear at a window, heard the crash
of rifles as the Apaches sent slugs ripping into the house.
Finally the Mexicans retaliated, but they fired wildly,
missing every time. Another volley from the warriors
elicited a strident scream. Then Delgadito spun and
retreated into the night.

Clay did the same. He was mildly surprised when the
Apaches turned westward instead of to the southeast.
Since talking was taboo when a war party was on the
go, he had to hold his tongue until they stopped in a
shallow ravine.

Delgadito came back and asked, "Were you hit?"

"I'm fine," Clay said in English. "Which is more than I
can say for all those you rubbed out without warning."

"You are upset? What did you expect?" Delgadito
inquired in his own tongue. "We are at war with the
Nakai-yes of Sonora. We did not choose to be at war
with them. They chose to be at war with us. Had they
been friendly, as were the *Nakai-yes* in Chihuahua, had
they not hired butchers to kill our wives and our children,
we would be content to leave them alone." He paused, his
face darkened by a rare display of emotion. "You were

there when Blue Cap attacked. You saw that, yet you condemn us for this?"

"No," Clay said in Apache, then added in English, "I reckon I can't."

"This is just the beginning. Before we are done, Sonora will run red with blood."

The vow was no idle boast. By morning the Apaches had attacked a hacienda, killing four men who put up a stiff fight, and burned out a farmer and his wife, shooting both in the head. Since there had been no recent reports of Apaches in the region, and since Apaches seldom attacked at night, the band had the element of surprise in its favor and met with little resistance.

It was a quiet and grim Clay Taggart who followed the warriors to their camp on the tableland and sat down with his back to a log. He felt tired, in body and soul, and he leaned his head on the log to rest.

"Are you still upset?"

Clay straightened and looked up at Delgadito. "Some. But not enough to raise a fuss. I realize you're doing what you have to do, so I'll keep my mouth shut and stay out of your way."

"You must do more."

"How do you mean?"

The warrior took a seat. Although he had been on the go all night long and had in fact been awake since the morning before, he showed no sign of fatigue. "You did not shoot once. You turned away when those last two were killed."

"They were farmers. The man did not even have time to grab a gun."

"They were enemies. You must stop thinking like a white man and start thinking like an Apache, if you are to help us." Delgadito placed a hand on Clay's knee. "It is easy if you try."

"And just how does an Apache think?" Clay asked without real interest.

"Our first and foremost business is staying alive. We know the *Nakai-yes* would wipe us out if they could, and we know the *Americanos* would do the same if their strange God would let them. The Pimas, the Comanches, the Kiowas all hate us and would kill us to the last man if they could catch us unawares. From the time we are born to the time we die, we must always be alert, always be ready to defend our lives. All men are our enemies. *All* men. This we are taught as soon as we can speak, and we know it to be the one truth that matters. The padres and the *Americano* reverends would have us treat all men as our brothers, to turn the other cheek, as they always tell us to do, but such ideas are for those who see the world as they would like it to be and not as it is."

The speech amazed Clay. He'd never heard the warrior talk at such length on any one subject before. "So you see everyone as your enemy. I understand that."

"But you do not *think* it. You do not think of the *Nakai-yes* as enemies. You must think of them as *your* enemies—"

"They're not," Clay broke in.

"What would they do to you if they caught you? What would your own people do to you if you fell into their hands?" Delgadito made a motion in disgust. "They would kill you, that is what they would do. Which makes them your enemies, just as they are our enemies. You have more in common with the *Shis-Inday* than you imagine."

Although Clay wanted to deny it, the truth stung. He told himself he could always leave the Apaches, leave

Arizona, and start all over. Provided, of course, Miles Gillett had not informed the Army he was the White Apache.

Clay reclined on his back, covered his eyes with a forearm, and fell asleep. It seemed like minutes later, but it was actually several hours later when a hand touched his elbow and he woke up to discover Cuchillo Negro at his side. The taciturn warrior pointed at a gap in the trees bordering their sheltered nook, where all the Apaches were gathered.

"I savvy," Clay said, then caught himself and said, "I will come see."

A company of Mexican cavalry was at the crossing watering their mounts. As Clay set eyes on them, he noticed a glint of sunlight move in a bright arc and immediately shouted in Apache, "Lie flat! Lie flat!" Suiting his actions to his words, he dove to the earth, then glanced up to see the warriors staring at him with mixed amusement and curiosity.

"What are you doing?" Delgadito asked. "They are too far away to see us."

"They have a—" Clay began, and had to stop because he had not been taught the Apache word for telescope.

"I always knew this white-eye was crazy," Fiero muttered.

"No," Clay said. He reverted to English and addressed Delgadito. "They have a telescope, a contraption that lets them see far, far away. From where they are they can spot us as plain as day."

"Tel-le-scope?"

"I don't know how to describe it. Just trust me. You have to get out of sight."

Suddenly the wail of a bugle shattered the mountain air. The cavalrymen were hurriedly mounting. There was much shouting and rattling of sabers.

"Too late," Clay said, rising. "They know we're here." Rotating, he surveyed the forested plateau. There was ample cover, but there were also enough soldiers to completely ring the top of the plateau and trap them on it. "We must find another way down, quickly," he advised.

Delgadito was skeptical. He had never seen nor heard of a telescope. By the same token, he had learned there were many wonderful devices used by the white-eyes and the *Nakai-yes,* such as the small round glasses that captured the power of the sun and turned it into searing fire. Grunting, he assumed the lead, bearing to the northeast.

Clay saw the cavalry galloping hard for the incline that would bring them to the top. Could the Apaches escape in time? He brought up the rear, his Winchester cocked, one eye on the rim. Twenty-five yards from it he bumped into someone.

"Take cover," Delgadito said.

The Apaches were fanning out, taking shooting positions.

"What are you doing?" Clay asked although their intent was obvious. "We should be lighting a shuck out of here, not making a stand."

"We know how the *Nakai-yes* fight, you do not," Delgadito responded. "Watch us and learn."

Clay immediately sought the trunk of a tree and braced his Winchester against it. The thunder of hoofs grew louder and louder; then suddenly the cavalry swept over the crest in a file of twos, going so fast they could not possibly stop or turn to evade the blistering rain of destruction that knocked them from their saddles as if they were targets in a shooting gallery.

Yipping and shrieking, the Apaches fired again and again. Impulsively, Clay joined in, working the lever smoothly, efficiently, banging off shot after shot. He dropped two, three, four troopers in twice as many seconds.

Again the bugle wailed. This time the milling, confused cavalrymen who had not been unhorsed raced frantically for the rim, fleeing even faster than they had arrived. More were knocked off their mounts. In moments those still able to retreat were gone.

Fifteen bodies lay in the dank grass, some twitching, some convulsing, others deathly still.

At a yelp from Delgadito, the Apaches swooped down on the wounded, dispatching one after the other with fierce abandon. A hefty trooper, blood trickling from a scalp wound, scrambled erect and attempted to run away. Fiero was on him in the blink of an eye, his knife biting deep. Another trooper was stabbed in the gut by Ponce. The slaughter was swift and violent.

Clay did not join in. He walked slowly toward the strife, feeding fresh cartridges into the Winchester. Out of the corner of an eye he detected movement and turned just as a cavalryman bearing a bullet hole in one shoulder sprang at him, aiming a wicked saber swipe at his head. In sheer reflex he brought the rifle up, deflecting the blow which was only the first of many.

The Mexican slashed madly, a feral gleam animating his face. Knowing he would die, that he didn't stand a prayer, the man was determined to sell his life as dearly as possible.

Clay had to backpedal. The saber was aimed at his head, his chest, his legs. One of the latter blows almost cut him off at the knees when he was a shade slow in jerking his legs out of the way. As it was, his moccasins were slashed.

So savage was the soldier's onslaught, Clay was unable to bring the rifle into play. He had to do something before the man drew blood, and the only thing he could think of was to hurl the rifle at the Mexican's face and draw a pistol. The ruse worked. Shifting to avoid the rifle, the cavalryman took a step to the right. Clay fanned the hammer, a trick he seldom used, snapping off four swift shots. At each one the soldier staggered backward, and on the fourth, he collapsed.

Whirling, Clay saw that all but one trooper had been disposed of, and Amarillo was tending to him. He retrieved the Winchester, then replaced the spent cartridges in the Colt. The saber of his fallen foe caught his eye, so he picked it up and hefted the weapon a few times. It had a nice feel to it. He would have liked to take it along but he already had more than enough weapons to carry and didn't care to be burdened with another.

Delgadito approached. "I saw you fight that *Nakai-yes*. You did well, White Apache."

"I didn't want to kill him."

The warrior changed to his own tongue. "He would have killed you. In his eyes you were his enemy. How long before you look at them as they look at you?" His tone held reproach. "All my words have flown through your head without stopping. I will tell you this one more time, and then whether you live or die is up to you." He paused for emphasis. "Think of them as your enemies. Think of all men as your enemies except the *Shis-Inday*."

Since the rifles of the cavalrymen were generally inferior to the Winchesters of the Apaches, the band did not bother to take any of the arms lying on the battleground. With one exception. An officer had been slain, and his pistol, a fine Schofield-Smith and Wesson .44 which he must have spent six months' salary on, was appropriated by Fiero, the warrior who had finished the officer off.

While the Apaches went from body to body, Clay went to the rim. The remnants of the patrol were in full flight to the northwest, toward Hermosillo. Riderless horses trailed in their wake. Clay was turning when he saw another Mexican lying halfway down the slope. The man bore a dark stain on his back, but he was still alive. As Clay watched, the trooper painfully crawled toward a clump of bushes to hide.

"The *Nakai-yes* are not worth counting."

The boast came from Fiero, who had come over and was openly admiring his new pistol.

Clay did not know what to say. It was rare for the firebrand to address him, rarer for Fiero to show him any friendliness whatsoever. So he did not quite know what to make of the warrior's remark.

"They are not true men. They fight like women," Fiero continued arrogantly. "We can kill them with rocks or our bare hands if we have to. When we tell of our exploits, we do not mention them because they are not worth counting."

"I would think you have killed very many," Clay said.

Fiero's chest swelled. "More than any of my people, yes. I toss the *Nakai-yes* around as a strong wind tosses dead leaves. They cannot stand before me."

"I am glad you are with us," Clay said, offering another compliment. Fiero swelled even more. Clay would have laughed had it not been a rank insult to do so.

"This is what I like best," Fiero declared, gesturing at the bodies. "I live to fight, as does any *Shis-Inday* worthy of the name. We are a warrior people, White Apache. We always have been, always will be. The white-eyes can force us on the barren reservations, can force us to lower ourselves to work the soil like the Pimas, but they can never take away the passion that burns in our hearts for our true way of life."

Clay had never heard Fiero speak so eloquently before, never been afforded so clear a glimpse into the other's innermost soul. He was at a loss to explain why the warrior had chosen that particular moment to open up to him, but since he wanted to be on friendly terms with every member of the band, he responded by saying, "If the *Shis-Inday* had more warriors like you, they would not be living on the reservations."

Fiero blinked, then grunted. "You speak true words, White Apache. *Palacio* and the other chiefs are like feeble old men. They are too afraid for their lives to resist any more. So, like trained dogs, they lick the feet of the reservation agents and the officers who treat them so shamefully." Fiero glowered. "*I* will never be like them! I will never let myself become a cur to please the white-eyes. I was born *Shis-Inday,* I will die as a *Shis-Inday.*"

Suddenly Fiero saw the trooper below, who had almost reached the weeds. "Look! Another one!" A single leap carried him over the crest, and he bounded down the slope like a mountain goat.

Clay did not stay there to see the Mexican dispatched. He walked to where Delgadito, Cuchillo Negro, and Amarillo were standing. "What do we do now?" he inquired.

"We head northeast," Delgadito said. "There we will

find many farms, many ranches. We will raid them
during the day and hide at night. In time, the scalp
hunters will come, and we will be ready."

"More killing," Clay said without thinking.

"War is killing," Delgadito responded. "And never
forget we are on the warpath and will stay on the warpath
until our land is once again our own. You saw us dedicate
ourselves during the dance."

How could Clay forget? The day before the band had
left Warm Springs for Mexico, the warriors had spent
the entire night in a ritual war dance around a roaring
fire. Clay had tried to sleep, but the constant beat of
Ponce's drum and the chanting of the others had kept
him up.

By the middle of the night Clay didn't mind all that
much. There had been something about the driving
rhythm that had gotten into his blood. He had sat up,
observing, swaying in time to the vigorous beat. Several
times he had nearly jumped up and joined them.

The war dance was as old as time itself. Moving
to the tempo of the drum, the four warriors lined up,
then slowly circled the fire four times. Afterward, they
divided into pairs, one pair dancing on the south side of
the fire, the second pair to the north. Later they shifted,
one pair going to the east, another to the west. Four
times they did this.

Next the warriors ringed the fire. Each one took turns
prancing around it, pretending to battle enemies he would
slay in the days ahead. Of them all, Fiero had leaped the
highest, chanted the loudest, danced the hardest. Secretly,
Clay had envied him.

"Yes, I saw," Clay now said.

"We must travel fast," Delgadito said. "We must strike
like lightning and never stay in one place for very long.

We are only six but they will think we are sixty."

The Apaches moved out, adopting a tireless dogtrot that ate up the miles quickly. Clay once again brought up the rear. So superbly conditioned had he become that he never once lagged. Had there been an onlooker to witness their passage, the onlooker would not have noticed any difference between the five bronzed warriors and the white man.

To all intents and purposes, it looked as if there were six Apaches on the warpath, not five.

Chapter Eight

The next week was to mark a turning point in Clay Taggart's life. A subtle change took place deep within him, so subtle he failed to realize that he had changed, and done so drastically, until after the fact.

On the first raid after the battle on the plateau, Clay stayed aloof, refusing to help butcher an old peon and the man's two sons.

On the second raid, made on a hacienda, Clay picked off several defenders from a distance with his Winchester.

On the third raid, a brazen attack on a large rancho, Clay helped hold off a party of vengeful *vaqueros,* shooting three of them with his pistols.

Then came the afternoon Ponce spotted a *conducta* bearing northward. The Apaches shadowed the wagon train until it stopped late that afternoon. The wagon master chose a poor spot: beside a stream where it formed a wide pool at the mouth of a narrow canyon.

The Apaches waited until twilight shrouded the land-scape before creeping down the canyon. Working their way from bush to bush, yucca to yucca, they drew within rock throwing distance of their prey. No mountain lion or jaguar could have moved more stealthily than they did.

Apaches were masters at this art. They could disguise themselves among brown shrubs, green grass, or gray rocks with equal ease, using whatever the terrain offered to blend into the ground, as if they were part of it. And where there wasn't enough grass or loose rocks or dirt, they were adept at contorting their bodies into the shapes of the objects around them. If they were moving through a boulder field, they would curl themselves into the shapes of boulders. If they were moving through yuccas they would mimic the appearance of the yuccas with the precision born of long experience.

Delgadito had taught some of these tricks to Clay, enough to permit Clay to approach the *conducta* without being detected. He saw the Mexicans going about the business of watering teams and cooking supper. Among them were a dozen or so women and children, and, on beholding them, Clay felt a twinge of regret. Then he reminded himself that these were the same people who had backed the government decision to place a bounty on Apaches, which made them partly responsible for all the Apache women and children who had been slaughtered by the scalp hunters. They deserved no mercy from him.

The Mexicans had just sat down to eat when Delgadito yipped, the signal for the attack. The single guard by the livestock dropped with a bullet through the brain. More men were shot as they rose or grabbed for guns. Panic reigned in the encampment, panic fueled by the war whoops and shrieks of the

Apaches, who made enough noise for twice their number.

Clay joined in, whooping at the top of his lungs while firing at targets as fast as they appeared; a driver who tried to aim an old carbine, a man in a fine suit who was shooting a derringer, another man who had climbed onto a horse and was about to ride off. A peculiar sense of excitement came over him, intense excitement of a kind he had never before felt. His heart beat madly, his blood pumped wildly. Had he looked into a mirror, he would have discovered a bloodthirsty grin on his face.

Fear aided the Apaches, fear so potent it drove many of the Mexicans fleeing into the night. Their horses and mules, their wagons, and their possessions were all forgotten in their haste to escape the dreaded terrors. A half dozen, however, showed real courage, forming a ragged line to cover the flight of their companions, shooting as they departed.

In the time a man could have counted to one hundred, the fight was over with the Apaches as undisputed masters of the *conducta*. They stalked into the circle of wagons warily, using their knives to end the lives of the wounded. Clay did not lend a hand. He was content to gather the horses which had not run off, and he was leading a sorrel to the middle of the encampment when a high-pitched scream brought him to a certain wagon on the fly.

Amarillo had found a woman and her boy of nine or ten years of age hiding under blankets. When Clay arrived, the woman and her son were huddled together by a front wagon wheel while the Apaches were debating their fate.

"—keep them for my own," Amarillo was saying.

"She has a healthy look about her. She will bear me many more sons."

"They could not keep up," Delgadito said. "You know the *Nakai-yes* are weaker than us. They would tire and have to be left behind."

"Then I will take the boy and kill the woman."

Fiero stepped forward. "Why waste her? Let us use her first before you slit her throat."

"It has been too long since any of us had a woman," Ponce mentioned, his dark eyes devouring the petrified mother. "We should draw straws to see who goes first."

Cuchillo Negro studied the pair a moment. "Are they worth one of us losing his life?"

"I have lost your trail," Amarillo said.

"What if those we drove off come back? What if there are soldiers in the area and they heard the shots?" Cuchillo Negro brought up.

"The ones we fought are too scared to return," Fiero declared. "And if *soldados* show, we will do to them as we did to those others six sleeps ago." He hefted his rifle. "Apaches do not run from Mexicans."

Clay had been staring at the woman. She had regained enough presence of mind to stop trembling and was glaring at her captors in undisguised hatred. A lesser woman would have been on her knees, in tears, begging for her life.

"I say it would be foolish to take them with us, and we do not have time for all of us to have our way with her," Delgadito declared. "Let us kill them both and be on our way."

"I disagree," Amarillo said. "Since I found them, I should have the final say."

"I side with Amarillo," Fiero stated.

Delgadito glanced from one to the other. "Since we cannot agree, I think we should ask our leader what to do."

Abruptly, all eyes were on Clay. He hesitated, debating what he should say. The woman meant nothing to him personally, but he was loath to harm either her or the boy. On the other hand, if he said as much, he would anger Amarillo and Fiero, just when they were starting to treat him with a little respect. Delgadito had put him on the spot, and he didn't like it at all.

"Well?" Fiero prompted.

Clay thought fast. "Amarillo is right," he said. "They are his to do with as he pleases. But Delgadito and Cuchillo Negro are also right. We are on the warpath, remember? You have taught me that, when on the warpath, an Apache always travels lightly and swiftly. We can do neither burdened with the woman and her child." He gave Amarillo his undivided attention. "We should leave them here and go. Later, after we have finished our business with Blue Cap, we can raid a small farm or two and find another woman for you. That would be fairest."

The Apaches shared looks. Amarillo pursed his lips, then replied, "There is wisdom in your words, Lickoyee-shis-inday. I will do as you suggest."

"And you, Fiero?" Clay asked.

"Amarillo caught them. Amarillo had decided." Fiero touched the knife on his hip. "But we cannot permit them to live or they will tell their friends how few we are." Before anyone could stop him, he took two rapid steps and plunged his blade into the mother's chest. Too shocked for words, she clutched once at Fiero's arm, then slumped against the wheel. Her son let out a wail and raised a fist to hit Fiero. The warrior was quicker.

Clay made no protest. He stared at the dead pair and wondered why he did not feel angry or sad over their deaths, why he did not feel *something*. Trying not to dwell on it, he pointed at the four horses. "We would make better time if we took them."

"We travel on foot when making war," Delgadito reminded him. "You know that. Horses leave too many tracks and are no good in mountainous country."

"I was thinking we could eat them later. We have been living off the land so long I have forgotten what a full meal is like."

"You are too soft," Delgadito said, grinning. "But so you will not starve, we should take one horse, no more. We must feast on it tonight and be elsewhere by morning."

Fiero ran to the fire and picked up a burning brand. "First we have this to do!" he cried, and dashing to a wagon, he set it ablaze.

The rest followed his lead. Clay gripped the unlit end of a burning stick, carried it to the wagon the woman and boy had been in, and tossed the stick inside. A bundle of blankets caught immediately, the flames feeding hungrily on the material. Soon they had spread to a crate containing clothes. The heat ignited the wagon itself.

Clay stood in the middle of the ring of burning wagons, among the corpses of those slain by the Apaches. With a puddle of blood inches from his feet, and the acrid scent of the smoke mingling in his nostrils with the pungent odor of blood, Clay Taggart raised his head to the heavens and whooped like the Apaches were whooping.

A strange, new, and intoxicating feeling took hold of Clay. He laughed long and hard, then danced in a circle while shaking his fists at the heavens. Never had he felt anything like this before, never had he felt so very thrilled to be alive.

The Apaches gathered at the pool. Everyone drank until they couldn't drink another drop, which was their custom when they knew it might be a while before they next tasted water. Fiero assumed the lead going up the canyon. Clay stayed next to Delgadito, who led the horse.

The war party climbed high into the mountains to a pocket of trees secluded from view from below. Here, a fire was built. Ponce and Amarillo killed the horse; then Cuchillo Negro joined them in carving off thick slabs of meat for their meals.

Clay sat on a flat stone listening to the crackle of the fire, his mouth watering at the tangy scent of the roasting flesh. There had been a time when he would have been sickened by the mere thought of eating a horse, but living among the Apaches had changed his outlook, and now he relished the taste as much as he did that of beefsteak.

The warriors talked in quiet voices of the events so far. Clay heard Blue Cap mentioned and shifted to catch the palaver.

"—stay in Sonora as long as we must to draw him into the open," Delgadito was talking. "It might take a moon; it might take two."

"Too bad we do not know where he stays when he is not out lifting hair," Cuchillo Negro said.

"A man like him never stays in one place too long," Clay said.

"I am more concerned about how many men he will have with him," Cuchillo Negro commented. "There could be more than twenty."

"They will be no match for us," Fiero said.

"If they were just white-eyes or *Nakai-yes*, I would agree," Cuchillo Negro responded. "But Blue Cap has many breeds in his band. Some are more Indian than white or Mexican. They can track almost as good as we can. If we are not careful, they will lead him right to us, when we are not ready for them."

"Then we must always be ready," Fiero said.

"If we knew when they were coming we could lay a trap," Ponce suggested.

"Blue Cap has not lived so long by being careless," Clay pointed out. "He is the best there is at what he does, so you can be sure he will attack when we least expect it."

"Let him!" Fiero growled. "I will rip his heart from his chest with my bare hands!"

The others, Clay noted, were not quite as confident. They had barely escaped with their lives the last time they tangled with Johnson, and there was no guarantee they would do so this time.

Soon all grim thoughts were banished. The meat was done, and each warrior ate with relish. Clay wolfed his down, as an Apache would, wiping the hot grease on his thighs. As he had done at the pool, he ate until he could not eat another morsel. When they were all done gorging themselves, the fire was extinguished; the leftover meat, buried.

Westward over a barren spine they traveled, the starlight barely enough for them to see more than a dozen yards with any clarity. Clay's full stomach made him drowsy. He resisted by shaking his head and pinching himself, aware that if he tripped or accidentally made any loud noise he would be looked down on by the others. Apaches took great pride in their wilderness skills. To earn their respect, he must prove their equal.

An hour later they halted in a dry wash. Clay was so tired that he was asleep the moment his head touched the ground. His full belly and the crisp air combined to give him the untroubled sleep of a baby, and he awoke refreshed and raring to go at first light.

The Apaches resumed their depredations. Two more ranchos were struck in swift succession over the next two days and a small traveling party was ambushed.

"Surely by now Blue Cap has heard we are here," Cuchillo Negro remarked as he sorted through the contents of a saddlebag. "All of Mexico must have heard about our raids."

"There is a way we could learn whether he has heard or not," Delgadito said, standing over one of the men they had just killed.

"How?" Clay asked.

For an answer, Delgadito stripped the dead man naked and held out the clothes. "Take these along."

"Why?" Clay asked suspiciously.

"So you can put them on when the time comes. With your features no one would think you were Apache. You can enter and leave as you please."

"Enter and leave what?"

"Sahuaripa. We will be there before nightfall."

"You want me to go into a town?"

"What better way to learn the latest news?" Delgadito rejoined, and tossed the clothes at Clay's feet. *"Habla español?"*

"Sì," Clay conceded. "A little."

"So do I, so we will go together."

"Do you want to die? They'll see you are an Apache and kill you on the spot."

Delgadito picked up a brown sombrero. "With this, a

pair of pants, and a serape I will look just like any other half-breed. No one will bother us."

The other warriors took the brainstorm as a matter of course, leading Clay to guess the brazen plan had been tried before, with success. For sheer gall it had no equal. The last thing the Mexicans would expect would be for Apaches to be wandering in their very midst.

It was dusk when their destination came into sight. Sahuaripa turned out to be a small pueblo of one hundred souls or so. A dusty track of a road wound westward from the town toward Hermosillo.

From a prominent ridge Clay surveyed Sahuaripa and did not like what he saw. There were too many people moving about. And he swore that he saw men in uniform among them. He made his concern known to Delgadito.

"We will be in little danger. The *Nakai-yes* pay no attention to breeds. Stay in the shadows, out of their way, and they will not even know you are there."

Although Clay's gut instinct warned him not to go along with the loco notion, he did so anyway. To back out would make the Apaches think he was yellow, and he wanted to show them he had as much sand as any man. The clothes he wore were a white cotton shirt, pants, and leather *huaraches*. A straw sombrero and a drab poncho served to hide his features and build tolerably well.

Delgadito wore the same, except his hat was brown, and his serape, a colorful mix of several hues. He shunned the *huaraches,* saying he preferred to go barefoot rather than wear the uncomfortable sandals.

The heavens had darkened to a dingy gray that matched Clay's gloomy mood when they descended the ridge to the road. They had waited until there were no travelers on it to avoid drawing attention to themselves.

Under Clay's shirt he carried both pistols and his knife. He unconsciously patted them for reassurance now and again as he strolled toward the town. The musical peel of big bells reached his ears, coming from a high church steeple at the north end of Sahuaripa.

"Remember to never look the *Nakai-yes* in the eyes," Delgaditio cautioned. "They bristle like porcupines if you do."

Most of the pueblo's inhabitants were heading toward the church. Clay veered from the road to the side of an adobe building and stopped to scan the single main street. A few men idled under overhangs. A few dogs were visible, all resting quietly. Near a house several children frolicked, laughing merrily. Sahuaripa was the perfect picture of serenity.

"Come," Delgadito said suddenly, advancing boldly into the street.

Tucking his chin to his chest, Clay followed, the skin at the nape of his neck prickling. He did not like this, not one bit. He was certain all eyes were on them, but when he braved a peek he found they were being totally ignored. Clay began to feel more confident until he saw where the warrior was leading him.

There was a drab cantina on the west side of the street. From its open doorway and windows wafted the soft music of a deftly played guitar. Two Mexicans lounged in front, talking.

Delgadito walked to the closest corner and squatted against the wall, pulling the brim of his hat down low, so no one could see his face. His keen eyes raked the street and found no cause for alarm. He noticed the worried look on his companion and nudged him with an elbow. "Do not be so tense," he whispered. "You will make others wonder."

"I'm trying," Clay said.

"Try harder," Delgadito directed. He was mildly annoyed that White Apache did not have more confidence in his judgment. They would be all right, as long as they did not make a mistake.

Overall, though, Delgadito had no complaints about the white eye's actions since leaving Arizona. White Apache had held his own, had behaved in a manner worthy of a true warrior, and Delgadito took a measure of pride in knowing he was largely responsible for the remarkable change that had taken place. When they had first met, White Apache had not been able to last two days on his own in the wilderness. Now, White Apache could live off the land as well as any *Shis-Inday*, and was slowly acquiring the skills that would make a seasoned warrior out of him.

Delgadito abruptly realized he had taken to thinking of the white eye as White Apache and not Clay Taggart. Another bad sign. He was definitely becoming too fond of the man, treating him like an oversized son rather than the enemy that he was. All whites were bitter enemies of the *Shis-Inday*. Every warrior knew that. So why was he finding it so hard to think of Taggart that way?

Clay could tell his friend was deep in thought and wondered what could possibly be so important at such a time. He cocked an ear toward the two Mexicans. His Spanish was rusty, but he gleaned enough to know they were talking about the current lack of rain and the threat to their crops if they did not get some rainfall soon.

Presently two more men approached. They were greeted by the pair near the door and the conversation turned to the recent raids by Apaches. Instantly Clay's interest perked up. So did Delgadito's.

"I have heard the army will send five compa-
nies to deal with the savages," one of the Mexicans
declared.

"What good will that do?" responded another.
"Apaches are not human. The army will not get so
much as a glimpse of them."

"*Sí,*" agreed the third man. "And have you noticed
how when the Apaches are reported in one area, the
army goes to another?"

There was laughter, and the first man said, "They
say the safest place to be when the Apaches are on
the warpath is with a patrol hunting for them."

More laughter. Then the quartet huddled closer.

"There is word that scalp hunters have been sent from
Hermosillo."

"Which bunch this time? Diaz's?"

"No. That gringo, the one they call Johnson."

"*Madre de Dios!* He is the worst of them all."

"*Sí.* There is a story that he once killed an Apache
woman and made a pouch from her breasts."

"Did you hear about the time he lined up nine or ten
Apache children in a row and then shot the first one
at close range to see how many his bullet would pass
through?"

"They say his favorite way to kill Apaches is to
hang them upside down over a fire and bake their
brains."

"I hope he does not come here. He treats us little
better than he does the Apaches."

"Do not worry. Captain Rivera will not let him abuse
us and our women."

"I guess there is a benefit to having the good captain
and his men quartered here. Although it is unfair for

us to have to feed and shelter them and not the government."

"Be quiet, Ramon. Here he comes."

Startled, Clay Taggart glanced up to see a stiff-backed young officer and a pair of burly soldiers, with rifles, walking briskly toward the cantina.

Chapter Nine

The officer looked directly at Clay, and Clay quickly averted his gaze, afraid the captain would see the color of his eyes and know he wasn't Mexican or a half-breed. Fortunately, the encroaching darkness worked in his favor. The officer marched into the *cantina* without so much as a word to the men outside.

Forgetting himself, Clay whispered in English, "We should skedaddle."

"The soldiers did not notice us," Delgadito replied in Spanish. "We will stay and learn more."

"How?"

"By going inside."

Clay plucked at the warrior's sleeve as Delgadito rose, but the Apache paid no attention, leaving Clay the choice of following or remaining there by himself. Irritated, Clay pretended to be interested in the wall as he walked to the doorway. The interior was dim, lit by a single lantern hanging behind the bar. Musty odors and low voices filled the room.

Captain Rivera and the soldiers were at the counter and had just been given glasses of tequila. The officer cast a casual glance at the entrance, then tipped his glass to his mouth.

Delgadito made for a secluded table in the darkest corner and sat facing the bar. Clay took a chair on the warrior's right, rested his elbows on the table, and, without being obvious, checked the patrons to see if any of them were staring. Not one man appeared at all interested in him or Delgadito.

"Be calm," the Apache whispered.

"What?" Clay said, hearing footsteps. He nearly jumped when a hand fell on his shoulder, and a bored voice addressed them.

"What will it be, senors?"

The barmaid was a plump middle-aged woman whose jowls hung clear past her chin. She made a halfhearted pass at the tabletop with a dirty cloth. "If you are hungry, I can have some enchiladas ready in five minutes."

"Whisky, *por favor*," Delgadito said with hardly any trace of an accent. Most Apaches could speak Spanish to a degree; he was especially fluent.

"*Lo mismo*," Clay said softly.

Without further comment she walked off. Clay let out the breath he hadn't realized he had been holding in and glared at the warrior. "You're plumb crazy!"

"I am not the one speaking English."

"How do you aim to pay for these drinks?"

Delgadito pressed a pocket and coins jingled. "One of the first lessons I learned about the *Nakai-yes* was the importance they placed on money. *Americanos* are the same. They value it more than life, which shows they do not know how to think properly."

A commotion at the bar drew Clay's interest. The young officer and an elderly townsman were having a disagreement, their words so loud as to be heard out in the street. All the customers stopped what they were doing to listen.

"I do not care if the government wants us to cooperate with those filth!" the elderly man snapped. "They are butchers, every bit as vile as the Apaches, and the good people of Sahuaripa will have nothing to do with them."

"When the government gives an order, we must obey," the officer said.

"You must because you are in the army. But we are private citizens and can do as we damn well please."

Captain Rivera set down his tequila. "Have a care, Pedro. The *presidente* would view your statements as treasonous, and you know what happens to those who lose his favor."

"My tongue will not be stilled!" Pedro said. "It is an outrage that we must harbor such killers! What is to stop them from abusing our women and bullying everyone else as they did in San Rafael?"

"My men and I will see that order prevails."

"There are only seven of you, and at last report Johnson had nineteen or twenty men riding with him. You will be unable to control him, and we will suffer the consequences."

"I repeat," Captain Rivera said testily. "My men and I will control him."

Pedro made a gesture of contempt and stalked from the *cantina*. Excited talk erupted in his wake.

"The *Nakai-yes*," Delgdaito remarked. "They love to chatter like squirrels."

Their drinks came. Clay sipped his, aware it would be the death of him if he let himself get booze blind and lose control. The drone of low talk and the coolness gradually relaxed him. After a while he cleared his throat and said, "How much longer will we stay here?"

"Are you in a hurry?"

"What else can we hope to learn? It's bad enough Johnson is on his way. We don't need more bad news."

"You forget the reason we came to Mexico. It is good news that Blue Cap is coming. Soon we will avenge our families. Then we can go back to our people with our heads held high."

"If you still have heads."

Delgadito pulled his sombrero a little lower. "Why is it you always look at the bad side of things? Are all white-eyes the same?"

"You call it looking at the bad side. I call it being realistic," Clay said. "You heard that man out front. I'm not partial to ending my days with my brains baked."

"Blue Cap only does that to Apaches. For you he would probably do something special, such as tie your legs to two horses and have the horses run in different directions."

"Thanks. That's a big comfort." Clay lifted the whiskey, and, as he did, he spied the officer staring in their direction. Involuntarily, he froze. Had the captain observed something unusual about them? He gulped, gritted his teeth as the fiery liquid burned a path to the pit of his stomach, and slid a hand under his shirt so he could grasp a revolver.

Captain Rivera tapped the bar a few times, his features thoughtful. He gave a nod, as if having just made up his mind, and started to advance toward the corner, his men in tow.

Over an hour earlier, about the same time that Clay Taggart and Delgadito were halfway to Sahuaripa, Fiero had risen below the crest of the ridge and announced, "I will hunt for our supper. Who wants to come with me?"

"I will," Ponce volunteered.

"Leave the fire to me," Amarillo said.

Cuchillo Negro made no comment. By the process of elimination he had to stay there and keep his eyes peeled, while the others attended to their tasks.

Fiero hiked westward into a gully. Because the sound of a gunshot could carry far if the wind was just right, instead of relying on his rifle, he picked up a rock the size of his fist. Shortly thereafter, he flushed a rabbit from some cactus. As was often the case with rabbits, this one ran a few yards, then stopped to look back and see if it was in any danger. A single, unerring throw brought it down, and Fiero was on the animal before it could stand and flee. His knife flashed once.

Ponce tried the same trick, but he was younger, less experienced, and he missed. Fiero, ready with another rock, caved in its skull.

Amarillo had a small fire crackling when the warriors returned. Ponce skinned the rabbits while Fiero climbed thirty feet to where Cuchillo Negro squatted.

"Has anything happened?"

"No. They went into the town, and all has been quiet since."

"That is a good sign," Fiero said.

"Don't tell me you are concerned for them?"

"For Delgadito, yes. We do not always see eye to eye,

but he is Apache. As for Lickoyee-shis-inday, I do not care if he lives or dies."

"So you say."

"What does that mean?"

"I have seen you talking to him more in the past few days."

"I talk to all of you."

"You would never speak a word to him before."

"I talked to a pony I had when I was but seven winters old, but that did not stop me from eating the pony later." Annoyed that anyone would dare think he could ever like a white-eye, Fiero descended to their camp and was greeted by the aroma of roasting rabbit. Ponce had already carved off a few chunks, poked a sharp stick through them, and propped the stick on a rock, so that the flames lapped at the juicy meat.

Kneeling, Fiero touched a finger to one of the chunks, then licked the blood off. He was ravenous, but he did not let on that he was. From childhood he had been taught to bend his body to his iron will, so no matter how hungry or thirsty he became, he would never show weakness by admitting as much. That was the Apache way.

Fiero was so close to the fire that when his ears registered a snapping noise, he thought it had been one of the burning branches. Then he heard something else, a soft scraping noise from the slope above him, and thinking that Cuchillo Negro had been unable to resist the smell of the food, Fiero twisted to chide him. What he saw brought a shout of warning to his lips, but he was too late.

Out of the twilight they swooped, from all directions at once, ten, twelve, fourteen, sixteen swarthy men who were on the three Apaches before the Apaches could so much as stand. The warriors tried to bring their weapons into play, but they were buried under an avalanche of pounding arms and driving fists.

Fiero got a hand on his knife, then lost his grip when a pair of hands gripped his arm and tore his fingers loose. Flat on his back, he was hit again and again and again. Helpless to resist, enraged at being taken so easily, he roared like a great, angry bear and tried to heave his attackers off. There were too many. They were too heavy.

The stock of a rifle streaked out of the mass of struggling men and struck Fiero full on the forehead. He sagged, tried weakly to fight back, and lost consciousness.

Captain Rivera had taken just a few strides when a tremendous racket exploded in the street. There were yells, oaths, and a scream that all mingled with the thuds of many hoofs. The patrons of the *cantina* rose to investigate. The officer spun, barked a few words to his men, then hastened out.

Delgadito stood and would have joined the mass exodus had Clay not grabbed his arm. "No. This way," Clay advised, leading the warrior to a side door. In all the fuss they were able to slip out and step to the fringe of the crowd that had gathered. More people were streaming from the church.

The cause of the uproar sat astride a splendid black stallion, a faded Union cap perched at a rakish ankle on his matted hair. A full, greasy beard framed his granite face, from which beady eyes glared at the world. Behind him sat more of his stripe, confirmed killers every one, outcasts who preyed on others for their livelihood.

"Blue Cap!" Delgadito exclaimed.

Ben Johnson was an imposing man. Tall, muscular,

and burnt to a chocolate brown by constant exposure to the sun, he appeared as formidable as the Indians he tracked down. Now he sneered at Captain Rivera and said in heavily accented Spanish, "I was told I could expect full cooperation from you. Can I?"

"*Sí*, senor. I have my orders."

"Good. Then you can sit on the prisoners until morning. I gave my word I'd get them to Hermosillo in one piece, more or less, and I don't aim to disappoint the governor."

"You have prisoners?" Captain Rivera asked.

"Three," Johnson said. "Caught up with them right outside your town, too. They must have been sizing up Sahuaripa in preparation for a raid." He rose in his stirrups and shouted, "Zapata! Haul their asses up here!"

The foremost scalp hunters moved their mounts aside, allowing Clay to see the captives. He inadvertently gasped and took a half-step, recklessly intent on helping them, but Delgadito's restrained him and whispered, "We would throw away our lives. Be patient."

Fiero, Ponce, and Amarillo were all bound at the wrists, their hands behind their backs. As an extra precaution, rope had been looped around their torsos from their elbows to their shoulders. All three warriors bore multiple bruises and smudge marks. Blood trickled from the corner of Ponce's mouth, while Fiero had a jagged gash on his brow that had stopped bleeding. They were hauled up to Rivera at the end of lariats by three scalp hunters, all breeds. In the lead was a stocky, scarred man who took delight in yanking his lariat so hard that Fiero stumbled and fell.

"Here they are," Johnson said. "By now I would have had their hair off and their heads roasting over a fire, but the governor wants to make an example of them. There's going to be a public execution, with everyone in Sonora invited."

"When will this be?" the officer inquired.

"Just as soon as I get them back to Hermosillo," Johnson said. "The governor is fixing to send out an invite to every town in the state. He wants the word spread far and wide so the damn Apaches will hear of it and get the message."

Clay and Delgadito had to stand helplessly as the three warriors were seized by some of Johnson's band and taken to a small, windowless shack, into which they were roughly shoved. A carpenter was called for and, on his arrival, instructed to nail a stout board across the door so that it could not be opened from either side. Next, Rivera posted three guards, issuing instructions for them to be relieved in the middle of the night by three others.

With the Apaches safely locked away, the citizens of Sahuaripa were in a festive mood. The curious trailed Johnson and company to the *cantina* and stood at the windows and door, peering in. The curious men, at any rate, because once it was known that the scalp hunters were in town, every last woman and child disappeared.

In the midst of the excitement, Clay Taggart and Delgadito stood unnoticed, by themselves, under an awning in front of a store.

"What do we do?" Clay asked. He could not quite get over the shock of the Apaches being caught. After all he had been through with them, he tended to regard them as more than human. It was a jolt to be so blatantly reminded they were flesh and blood and not invincible.

"Help them escape," Delgadito answered. He, too, was shocked; he had not thought anyone capable of taking the band by surprise when they were on their guard. This was one of the few times in his life he did not know what to do next, which was exactly what White Apache was asking.

"How?"

"I do not know yet, but there must be a way."

"They should be safe until they reach Hermosillo," Clay said. "Which gives us some time to come up with a plan." He glanced at the shack and reverted to English again. "I don't like the odds. Maybe we'll have to whittle them down before we show our hand."

"We will come back later. Right now we must leave."

"What? Why?"

"Do you know how to use your eyes?" Delgadito asked in Spanish. "Cuchillo Negro was not with them."

An empty side street brought them to the open country flanking the town on the south. In the distance a coyote howled. Behind them raucous laughter and gruff voices rose on the breeze.

They went a hundred yards, then stripped to their breechcloths and hid their clothing in a clump of dense brush. At a dogtrot they headed for the ridge, availing themselves of whatever cover was to be had.

The wily Delgadito made a circuit of the immediate area where he had left the others before venturing nearer, so as not to blunder into a trap. It would have been in keeping with Blue Cap's past practices to have left some men behind to ambush any Apaches who showed up later.

Only when convinced there were no scalp hunters lurking in the vicinity did Delgadito go forward. The lingering scent of wood smoke guided him to the spot where the fire had been built. This he rekindled, and taking a brand, he roved about reading the sign.

Clay could tell there had been a tremendous fight, but little more. He was not yet adept enough to determine how many men had been involved or to deduce the sequence of events. He found a dirty strip of cloth that must have been torn from the shirt of one of the scalp hunters and showed it to the warrior. "What do you think?"

"Fiero, Ponce, and Amarillo were at the fire when Blue Cap's men took them unawares," Delgadito said.

"I did not think that was possible," Clay confessed.

"They were careless," Delgadito said, walking in an ever widening circle. "They were too close to the fire and could not hear the sounds around them. They were looking into the flames, instead of away, so their eyes were not adjusted to the dark." He kicked at the ground, raising a puff of dust. "This is what comes of being too sure of yourself."

"What about Cuchillo Negro?"

"I have—" Delgadito began and abruptly stopped, his head snapping up.

Clay heard it, too, a scraping sound from a dozen feet away. He whirled, drawing a pistol, and spied a figure heading toward them. Just as he was tightening his finger on the trigger, the figure lurched, stumbled, shuffled on.

"Cuchillo Negro!" Delgadito declared, racing to the warrior's aid. Cuchillo Negro's head drooped, his arms hung limply. Blood seeped from a wound in his head, down across his neck and over his chest. Delgadito hooked an arm around the other's waist and bore him to the fire, where he gently laid Cuchillo Negro down.

An examination revealed the wound was deep, that Cuchillo Negro had lost much blood. If the wound had been any deeper, it would have proven fatal. Cuchillo Negro's eyes were closed for a while. They fluttered open finally and he looked up at them. "The others?"

"Blue Cap took them," Delgadito said.

"We must save them," Cuchillo Negro said. Feebly, he tried to rise but was unable to muster the strength. He sank down with a scowl.

"There is time," Delgadito told him. "You must rest. We will make you well again."

Cuchillo Negro touched his wound and winced. "It was a breed who hit me. I did not hear him until he was almost on me."

"We will talk about it later."

"I was on the very top," Cuchillo Negro said. "When he struck I fell over the side. I remember tumbling a long way."

"Rest now."

Cuchillo Negro did not seem to hear. "I think I also remember them searching for me. There were voices, and I saw men moving around." He stopped, his eyelids slowly closing. "I wanted to help the others but I could not. That is the last I recall." His head sagged to one side. His mouth parted once more, but all that came out was a long, deep breath. He had passed out.

"I will bring water and plants to make medicine," Delgadito said. "You keep watch."

"Do you think there is any chance Johnson will come back?"

"He has what he wants."

Clay watched the Apache vanish into the darkness, then sat with his back to the fire, the pistol in his lap. He'd rather have a rifle, but he'd left his Winchester behind when he went into Sahuaripa. So had Delgadito, which meant both guns were now in the hands of the scalp hunters.

The raid had turned into a disaster. The hunters had become the hunted. Clay was all for lighting a shuck for the border at first light. But they couldn't, not with Cuchillo Negro unable to go anywhere and the others in the hands of Ben Johnson.

What else could go wrong? Clay wondered. He knew the answer well enough: anything and everything. Given the pattern of his life of late, he had to be ready for the worst. Lilly. Gillett. The lynching. Now this. If he didn't know better, he'd swear someone had put a hex on him. He wasn't the superstitious sort, though. He was just having the Godawfullest string of luck in the history of the Southwest.

The cool breeze on Clay's toes made him think of his moccasins. They also had been left behind since no one but Apaches wore footwear of that kind. He rose to see if perhaps the scalp hunters had not bothered to take them. He should have known better.

Feeling disgusted, down at the mouth, Clay paced to stay awake and keep alert. His stomach grumbled, but he paid it no mind. He was occupied with troubling recollections of Ben Johnson's attack on the Apache camp back in the States weeks ago, an attack that had been swift, precise, and thorough, showing that Ben Johnson wasn't the type of *hombre* to leave anything to chance. Which made Clay suspect that, sooner or later, some of the scalp hunters would return to look for Cuchillo Negro. Or, rather, for Cuchillo Negro's hair, worth forty dollars in bounty money.

Clay hoped Delgadito would not take very long. He grew impatient when an hour dragged by, and then two. Hoping to spot the warrior approaching, he climbed to the top of the ridge and surveyed the benighted country-side. There was movement, but not where he expected to see it. Down on the road were two riders, barely visible, trotting westward. As they came abreast of the ridge, the very spot where the ambush had taken place, they angled into the brush and came on at a gallop.

Clay didn't need to see them clearly to know they were scalp hunters.

Chapter Ten

Surprise rooted the White Apache to the spot. But galvanized into action by the sudden thought of what the killers would do to him if they caught him, Clay Taggart spun and flew down the slope. Quickly he scooped handfuls of dirt onto the small fire, extinguishing it. Kneeling, he got his hands under Cuchillo Negro's broad shoulders and proceeded to drag the warrior off. All the time his ears strained to their utmost. He knew when the scalp hunters had started up the ridge by the heavier steps of their mounts; he knew when they were nearly to the rim by the loud clattering of loose earth and stones.

By then Clay was forty feet from the camp among waist-high boulders. He shielded Cuchillo Negro behind one, palmed both revolvers, and crept to a gap.

The scalp hunters had reined up at the crest. Both had rifles in their hands; both had an air about them of professionals who dispensed death as readily as most men breathed. They rode side by side down to where smoke curled skyward from the dead fire.

"It should have been plumb cold by now," the taller of the pair remarked.

"Maybe an ember caught," said the second man. "Fernando only kicked a little dirt on it."

"That damn breed can't do anything right. None of them can."

"Don't let them hear you say that, Blyn, or Zapata will stick a blade between your shoulders, when you're not lookin'."

"I'm not scared of him."

"You should be. He's as loco as a rabid wolf and as tetchy as a teased sidewinder. I wouldn't want him after me."

"That's 'cause you're the careful type, Jessup. I'm not."

The man named Jessup swung down, ground hitching his bay. "Let's get this over with so we can mosey on back and bend our elbows at that *cantina*. I've got me a powerful thirst for more coffin varnish."

"I don't see why Johnson had to send us," Blyn complained, dismounting.

"We were the only ones half sober."

"I don't see why this couldn't have waited until morning."

"When the boss says go fetch a scalp, we go fetch a scalp," Jessup said. "Just between you and me, I figure he was tryin' to impress that chili-eater captain by showin' how he could throw his weight around."

"He should have thrown it at somebody else."

"Hobble that lip of yours and let's get to lookin'," Jessup said, his rifle leveled as he moved upward. "That redskin has to be around here somewhere. We didn't see him on the other side comin' up."

"Most likely he crawled into a hole to die," Blyn said. "These Injuns are just like animals that way."

"Wherever. Just so we find him. We go back empty handed, Johnson is liable to take a cut out of our share."

"He wouldn't."

"Like hell. He'll deduct the bounty on one scalp from the money we have comin'."

"I don't like that. It ain't fair. We've worked as hard as everyone else. We're entitled."

Jessup stopped and turned. "Enough. I've never met an *hombre* so afflicted with diarrhea of the jawbone. You Texans beat all. Now hush and let's do what we were sent to do."

Clay had noticed that the killers slurred a few words. They showed no signs of being roostered, though, and he had no doubt they were as deadly as they were stone sober. Eventually the hard cases would scour the whole area, and they were bound to check the boulders, so, once they were far enough off, he wedged the Colts under his breechcloth and began dragging Cuchillo Negro farther south.

Clay should have kept on going, should have put all the distance he could behind him, only he kept thinking of those two horses. He knew that escaping Johnson's vicious pack on foot would be impossible. With the horses, the Apaches might pull it off.

Sixty yards from the camp was a gully. Clay left the wounded warrior after covering him with brush; then, on cat's feet, he stalked toward the scalp hunters. He spied the horses first and eased onto his hands and knees. Like a lizard he crawled on, his knife in his right hand. He would freeze every few feet to look and listen, as Delgadito had taught him.

The bay and the calico were nipping at what little grass was available. Only the bay looked up, and it uttered no sounds.

Clay skirted them to the west, his gaze roving the skyline and the slope. He was certain the renegade Texan, Blyn, was in that particular area, but he failed to spot him. Stopping beside a bush, he did as an Apache would do and curled his body in the same shape so that it appeared there were two bushes, not one.

Suddenly a low cough broke the deceptive tranquility.

Twisting, Clay looked to his left and was amazed to see Blyn seated on a boulder, not quite ten feet away. The Texan had his back to Clay and was fiddling with his boots.

Clay hesitated. Here was the ideal chance. But he had never killed a man in this fashion before, and he was unsure of himself. Girding his courage, he rose into a crouch and closed on the unsuspecting scalp hunter. His palm felt sweaty, his mouth was exceptionally dry. He would have licked his lips if he had not been too tense to move his tongue.

A yard, no more, separated Clay from the boulder, and he was raising his knife arm when Fate reared its ugly head and Blyn abruptly stood and turned. Their eyes met. The Texan vented a curse and whipped his rifle up, working the lever in a smooth motion.

Clay was faster. In one bound he alighted on the boulder, then lunged, catching Blyn around the waist and bearing the scalp hunter to the hard ground. The rifle went off, banging in Clay's ear, the blast deafening. Clay stabbed at the Texan's side but Blyn blocked the blow with a forearm and drove his knee into Clay's groin.

Sputtering, in agony, Clay shoved to give himself room to use his weapon. It proved to be a mistake. It gave the scalp hunter the opportunity to swing his rifle, the stock clipping Clay on the temple, knocking him flat.

Blyn, on his knees, swung the rifle overhead to bash Clay's head, but Clay rolled, and the rifle glanced off his left shoulder. Both men scrambled to their feet, Clay darting in and flicking the knife. Blyn retreated, using the rifle to counter Clay's thrusts.

The Texan unexpectedly hopped to the right, beyond the radius of Clay's swings, and pumped the rifle lever. Clay leaped, swatting the barrel as it was trained on him. Blyn got a hand on his wrist, and together they toppled.

Locked nose to nose, the two men grappled, each seeking to gain an edge. Blyn tried to bend Clay's wrist to force Clay to let go of the knife while Clay gouged his fingers into Blyn's throat. The Texan jerked his head back and retaliated by smashing a fist into Clay's jaw.

Pinpoints of light danced before Clay's eyes. He shrugged off the blow and lashed out, trying to return the favor, but Blyn thwarted him. Blyn seized his other arm, and they rolled back and forth, deadlocked.

Clay struggled to wrest his arms loose, without success. It seemed to him that the Texan wasn't trying all that hard to kill him and was instead content to hold fast to his arms. The reason dawned on him with startling clarity: Blyn was counting on Jessup to show at any second and lend a hand.

Redoubling his efforts, Clay got one arm loose and smashed the scalp hunter on the cheek. Blyn tried to grab his arm, but missed. Swiftly, Clay reached up, switched the long knife from one hand to the other and speared the blade at Blyn's throat. The steel bit into the fleshy part of the Texan's shoulder, as Blyn threw himself backward.

Clay shoved upright. The scalp hunter did the same. They circled one another, Blyn glancing at the rifle lying between them. Blyn feinted a grab for the gun, and when Clay sliced at his hand, he shifted, dropped his other hand to his boot and straightened holding his own knife, an Arkansas toothpick several inches longer than Clay's.

The Texan now had the advantage. A skilled knife fighter, he sneered wickedly as he drove Clay steadily backward. It was all Clay could to do keep from being cut. He parried as best he could, their blades clashing, ringing like tiny bells.

At any moment Jessup would arrive. Clay anticipated a slug or a knife in the back, and he was sorely tempted to risk a glance or two over his shoulder. When he saw the scalp hunter's eyes go beyond him, he could no longer stand the suspense. Taking a rapid stride to one side, he pivoted. But no one was there. It had been a trick.

Clay brought his knife higher just as Blyn pounced. Again their blades clashed. Blyn clamped a hand on Clay's throat, looped a leg behind Clay's ankle and shoved. They smacked down, the Texan on top.

Searing pain lanced Clay as the scalp hunter's knife dug into his flesh. Automatically he pushed with all his might, then scrabbled frantically to the left. His right leg was nicked, drawing blood. A chop at his ankle had missed by a hair. Executing a flip, Clay rose and bent at the middle to present a smaller target.

Blyn stabbed again and again, never leaving himself open for a counterthrust. High, low, short thrusts, long thrusts—he tried them all.

So savage was the attack, Clay was unable to draw a pistol. That is, until the scalp hunter drove the Arkansas toothpick at Clay's groin. Clay hopped backward so that the point of the knife only brushed his breechcloth while, at the same time, his left hand swooped to a revolver. The Texan looked up, looked right into the barrel of the Colt, and tried to hurl himself to the left.

Clay snapped off two shots, the first coring Blyn's forehead and causing the tall Texan to stumble, trip, and start to fall as the second shot ripped into his chest. Catapulted into a cactus, Blyn bounced off and fell, face first. His fingers twitched a few times, then were still.

Clay needed a breather, but Jessup was still unaccounted for. Rotating, he did a double take on confronting a stout form nearby, a form that materialized into Delgadito. "There's another one hereabouts!" Clay said. "We have to make wolf meat of him before he goes and tells Johnson!"

"No need," the Apache said, holding out his right hand. Blood dripped from his knife. "He was in such a hurry to get here he did not see me."

Clay slowly straightened, the tension draining from his body. "You took care of him," he said gratefully.

"I was on my way back when I heard a gunshot," the Apache disclosed in his own tongue. "I came running and saw him."

"What the hell took you so damn long?" Clay demanded in English.

"I explain later. Now we must go. Someone in town maybe hear shooting," Delgadito answered in the same language.

Clay grabbed Blyn's rifle and led the way to the horses. The bay gave them no problems, but the calico shied and would have bolted if Delgadito hadn't seized the reins and spoken softly while stroking its neck. In a minute, the horse calmed. Mounting, they galloped to the gully. Clay uncovered Cuchillo Negro and, working with Delgadito, carefully draped the unconscious brave over the back of the bay.

Swinging up, Clay was about to head to the southwest when Delgadito told him to wait and sprinted into the night. Clay nervously tapped his fingers, knowing that no true Apache would be so fidgety but unable to help himself.

Delgadito shortly returned bearing, of all things, a canteen and a small bundle wrapped in a cloth.

"Where the dickens did you get those?" Clay asked.

"The canteen I found in Sahuaripa."

"You went into town?"

"I did not have anything in which to carry water so I took it off of Blue Cap's horse," Delgadito explained matter-of-factly.

"You didn't!" Clay blurted. Had a white man made such a preposterous claim, Clay would have suspected it was a joke. Apaches, however, never indulged, at least, not in that sense. On remembering this, he threw back his head to laugh long and hard.

"Let us go."

Clay wanted to ask about the bundle, but the next half an hour was spent in flight, and he was too preoccupied with avoiding obstacles and holes to waste breath by talking. Riding at night, especially on a moonless night, was always dangerous. Delgadito took him on a confusing course over hill and down dale—first bearing westward, then southward, then to the east for a brief spell before heading southwest—always sticking to the rockiest ground, never riding the high lines.

When they eventually halted, Clay had no idea where they were, except to know they were on top of a low bluff flanking a stark mountain. In order to insure the bay didn't stray off, he tied its reins to a yucca.

Delgadito was unwrapping the bundle when Clay walked over. Inside were various plants, some Clay had never seen before.

"Herbs for a poultice?"

"Poul-tice?"

"Something to put on his wound to make him better."

"Yes."

A fire was built, a tiny one hidden by a ring of stacked rocks. Delgadito hurried away, showing up presently with a crude bowl carved from tree bark. Into this he mixed pieces of the plants, adding water and mashing them to the consistency of a thin paste. This was applied liberally to Cuchillo Negro's head. "Now we wait," Delgadito said.

"What about the others?"

"We must think of a plan to save them," Delgadito said. "In the morning. We need rest." So saying, he reclined on his back, covered his eyes with an arm, and fell asleep instantly.

Clay gawked, dumfounded the warrior could sleep so effortlessly with them in such a fix. He tried to follow the warrior's example but was too high-strung to nod off. Rising, he walked along the rim of the bluff, admiring the heavenly spectacle. Once he located the North Star, he had a fairly good idea of where they were and wasn't taken aback when he spotted the lights of a town to the northeast. The crafty Delgadito had brought them nearly full circle, to within a mile of their previous camp site. The town was Sahuaripa.

A shooting star flared in the sky to the southeast, arcing earthward in a blaze of light. Clay watched and recalled an old family belief that shooting stars were a good omen. He hoped so. The way things were going, he could use all the luck thrown his way.

At last Clay felt tired enough to lie down. Cuchillo Negro was sleeping peacefully and did not feel warm to the touch. Clay made a mental note to ask Delgadito more about the plants used in the poultice in the morning.

It was a hand on Clay's shoulder that awakened him. As he opened his eyes, another hand covered his mouth and lips touched his ear.

"Make no noise, White Apache. Some of Blue Cap's men are very close."

The sky to the east bore pale shades of pink, showing that dawn was not far off. Clay got on his hands and knees and crawled beside Delgadito to the north rim. He could see Sahuaripa in the distance, smoke curling lazily from a number of the buildings. Below the bluff was something he had not spotted the night before: the road to Hermosillo. Six scalp hunters had stopped there so one of their number could check a shoe on his mount. Their voices were borne upward by the breeze, faint but understandable.

"—wouldn't want to be the redskins who killed Jessup and Blyn when Johnson gets ahold of them."

"Yep. Did you see his face when that smart aleck officer told him we must not be as tough as everyone thinks?"

"Lordy. I figured he was fixin' to tear into that upstart and have him for breakfast."

"He got even, though. That officer ain't none too pleased about havin' to help."

One of the riders glanced at the man checking the shoe. "Are you done yet? Hell, we could have made a new one and put it on by now."

"Come on, Stevens!" prompted another. "We got us a

wide area to search and we have to be back in Sahuaripa by noon."

In moments they were on the road westward.

Delgadito squatted and watched the dust cloud recede. Most of the words he had understood, and he had learned enough to deduce that most or all of the scalp hunters and the solders were out hunting for them and would be out hunting until midday. And if that were the case, only a few men had been left in town to guard the prisoners. There would be no better time to try and rescue them. "I must go," he announced, easing back from the edge.

"Go where?" Clay inquired.

Delgadito explained while wiping dust from the rifle he had taken from the scalp hunter he had killed the night before.

"It's too risky a proposition for just one man," Clay protested. "Both of us should go."

"One of us must stay with Cuchillo Negro."

Clay looked at the wounded warrior. Delgadito was right. But only Delgadito knew enough about herbs and healing to help Cuchillo Negro. "You're the one who has to stay with him. I'll go instead."

"Why you?"

Clay told him, adding, "They might be expecting a stunt like this so they'll be on the lookout for anyone who looks suspicious. Since I don't have a lick of Indian blood in me, they won't pay me any mind."

Delgadito did not like the idea even though it made a lot of sense. "You would do this thing for Fiero and Ponce, who do not like you all that much? For Fiero, who would have killed you if not for me?"

"I gave my word back in the States, and I aim to stand by it," Clay said. "I'll settle with Fiero, once and for all, after we're out of this mess."

"You are a good man, Lickoyee-shis-inday," Delgadito said, and meant it. His people, by their very nature and upbringing, were inclined to put their own welfare above all other considerations. Self-sacrifice was rare. For a man to risk his own life to save others was viewed as foolish. Any warrior who died on the field of battle so that others might live was mocked. Delgadito, himself, was willing to go into town after the three warriors simply because if they died he would never be able to regain a position of leadership among his people. The raid must be a success. Every last warrior must return alive.

As Delgadito watched White Apache prepare, he began to realize that there was more to the white-eye than he had believed. The man was willing to sacrifice himself for his enemies. Such a startlingly new concept made Delgadito's mind whirl. And, despite himself, he felt his respect for the white man growing by leaps and bounds.

Had Delgadito been privy to Clay Taggart's thoughts, his admiration would have dimmed. The sole reason Clay had volunteered was his conviction that without the help of the captured men the band stood little chance of reaching the border alive. There was strength in numbers; they needed to be at full strength to prevail over the scalp hunters.

Presently, Clay jogged eastward. He went on foot to reduce the odds of being spotted, using the terrain as the Apaches would, avoiding open tracts where possible. Acting on the assumption the scalp hunters and soldiers were off in the hills, he paralleled the road where the going was easy. Twice he had to hide when riders appeared. Both were Mexicans on their way to Hermosillo.

Clay found the spot where their clothes were hidden without difficulty. Screened in a thicket, he donned the pants, shirt, poncho, and sombrero. This time, rather than leave the rifle behind, he wrapped it in the serape Delgadito had worn. The gun under his arm, he then hiked into town.

Tantalizing food smells filled the air. Few people were as yet abroad. A dog walked stiff legged toward Clay, its neck hairs bristling, but ran off when Clay kicked dust at it.

By taking one side street after another, Clay went to the north side of the shack in a roundabout manner. There were only two guards, both *soldados,* who were having a hard time staying awake. Apparently they had been on duty most of the night.

Clay hunkered down at the corner of a building and pondered what to do. He had to dispatch the guards quietly to gain time to cut the three warriors loose. Otherwise, the enraged Mexicans would be on them in a flash. And he had to do something soon, before the citizens of the town were out and around.

One of the guards said something to the other and walked away. The remaining soldier commenced walking around the shack, rifle angled over a shoulder.

Clay waited until the first guard was out of sight and rose. He guessed the man had gone to relieve himself or to buy breakfast. In either event, Clay didn't have much time. He ambled toward the shack, making a show of not being the least bit interested in it. When the remaining soldier disappeared around a corner, Clay ran to that corner, unwound the serape from his rifle, tossed the serape aside, and then hurried to catch up with the soldier so he could slam the rifle stock on the man's head.

His plan had just one unforeseen flaw.

The *soldado* had turned around and was walking toward him.

Chapter Eleven

To the soldier's credit, he did not question Clay's identity or ask what he was doing there. The soldier took one look at the rifle and brought his own to bear.

But before he could fire, the White Apache was on him, swinging his rifle in a powerful arc. The stock crashed onto the soldier's skull, and the man dropped and lay as still as death with blood seeping from his split skin. Clay did not waste time checking to see if the soldier were still alive. He had a more important task to perform.

Dashing to the door, Clay pried at the board with his fingers. It didn't budge so he drew his knife and wedged the tip underneath it. Prying vigorously, he worked the right end of the board outward. The nails rasped loudly, and he glanced around to insure no one had overheard.

That was when Clay saw the boy. A child of nine or ten was gaping at him as if he were the Devil incarnate. He offered a friendly smile and went back to work. A minute later, the boy was gone.

Clay swore and redoubled his efforts. The boy was bound to spread the alarm. In two to three minutes the area would be swarming with armed men.

Once Clay got his fingers under the board and braced a leg against the wall so he could exert more force, the board came off quickly. Clay threw the door wide and said, in Apache, "Come out! Hurry! They will be on us soon!"

Fiero stumbled through the doorway first, blinking in the bright sunlight. The others followed. All three were smudged with dirt.

"You!" Fiero exclaimed. "I thought it would be Delgadito or Cuchillo Negro."

"No time to explain," Clay said, slashing the ropes that bound the firebrand's arms. Next he cut the ropes around Fiero's wrists and shoved the knife into Fiero's hands. "Here. Do the rest while I keep us covered."

Angry shouts indicated a mob was on the way. Clay darted to the nearest junction and saw a score of armed men advancing. The little boy was among them. On spying the White Apache the mob let out a collective howl and ran forward, but only a few yards. Clay whipped his rifle up, and they all made for cover. One snapped off a wild shot.

Clay hurriedly backpedaled to the shack. Fiero had freed Ponce and was working on Amarillo. Ponce suddenly shouted and pointed to their right. Spinning, Clay saw the other soldier, just as the man fired. The slug buzzed past, smacking into the shack. Clay responded without thinking, and his aim was more accurate.

"Which way?" Fiero cried.

Breaking into an eastward run, Clay turned right and sprinted between a pair of buildings. At the far corner he stopped and glanced toward the main street. The mob was regrouping. Taking a breath, he sped across the next street to the building beyond. The Apaches tried to cross without being seen too, but only Fiero had made it when vicious shouts erupted and the mob surged toward them.

"Run!" Clay bellowed, doing exactly that. His sandals slapped the ground so hard his soles stung. He discarded the sombrero and shrugged out of the uncomfortable poncho. Three more dusty streets were crossed; then open country lay before them.

Clay slowed down, motioning for the warriors to precede him. They took off like antelope, making for a hill to the south. Clay glued his eyes to the street they had vacated, and, moments later, the mob appeared. To discourage his pursuers, he snapped off a shot over their heads. It would have been child's play to drop one or two, but if he fired into their midst he risked hitting the little boy.

The mob scattered, men diving for shelter wherever they could find it. One man dove through the open window of a house, and there was a strident scream.

Clay congratulated himself. The rescue had gone much better than he had expected. The Apaches were safe and unharmed and none of Sahuaripa's citizens seemed interested in giving chase. Then Fiero shouted and pointed to the west. Shifting, Clay felt his blood chill and aired his lungs a blue streak.

Five scalp hunters were bearing down on them at a gallop. Every last man had his rifle shucked, and each seemed eager to be the first to drop one of the warriors.

Clay slanted to the right to put himself between the cutthroats and the Apaches. The range was too far for

a precise shot, but he fired anyway, elevating the barrel
a bit to compensate. No one was more surprised than
he was when one of the killers flew from the saddle
as if smashed by an invisible fist. The rest immediately
looped to the north.

The Apaches reached the hill, raced up and over.
Clay wondered if they were deserting him and didn't
hold it against them if they were. In their eyes he
was a hated white-eye, nothing more. Expendable, as
the army might say. But he was sorely disappointed.
He'd expected better treatment after pulling their fat out
of the fire.

Running smoothly, Clay received a second surprise at
the top of the hill. The warriors were crouched on the
other side, awaiting him.

Fiero, grinning fiercely, yipped and declared, "That
was a fine shot, White Apache! I have never done better
myself!"

About to admit that it had been a sheer fluke, Clay
changed his mind. He had been trying too hard for too
long to earn their respect. So what if he had killed
that hard case more by accident than design? The only
way to impress Apaches was to prove their equal—
or their better—in things that mattered most to them,
such as warfare. "One less killer of Shis-Inday women
and children," he said modestly.

"Where is Delgadito?" Ponce asked.

"Waiting for us," Clay answered, "but we must be
careful not to lead the scalp hunters to him. Cuchillo
Negro is hurt and cannot be moved."

"What would you have us do?" Fiero asked. "You
have done well, and I, for one, will do as you want."

Clay would not have been more shocked if the Second
Coming had just taken place. To hide his astonishment,

he busied himself passing out weapons: a pistol to Fiero, a pistol to Amarillo, and his knife to Ponce. "I'll need them back later," he said. Stepping to the crest, he discovered the scalp hunters were now to the northeast, circling the hill slowly.

"Come," Clay said, pivoting on a heel. He sprinted down the slope toward the highland, where they would find sanctuary. Once they lost their pursuers he would guide the warriors to Delgadito.

The killers had other ideas. They came around the hill on the east, staying just out of rifle range, dogging the band.

Clay stared at them, gauging whether to try another shot. Suddenly he noticed there were only three men, not four. Where was the other one?

A puff of dust to the west provided the answer. The last man was on his way to find Ben Johnson and the rest of the scalp hunters.

"Damn!" Clay snapped.

The Apaches looked in the same direction and came to the same conclusion. They picked up the pace without being asked to do so, impervious to the blistering sun that baked their tanned forms.

Clay paused twice, once to remove his shirt, the other to remove his baggy pants. It felt wonderful to be in his breechcloth again, to feel the wind on his body. He would have discarded the sandal, too, except his soles were not as accustomed to traveling over rough terrain as were those of the Apaches.

For the better part of an hour the stalemate held. The trio of scalp hunters made no rash attempts to stop the Apaches. They were content to hang back and await reinforcements.

Clay began to think he had spared the warriors from

one grisly fate only to place them in graver jeopardy. Ben Johnson might not be so inclined to capture them alive a second time, governor or no governor. All the scalp hunters needed to do was completely surround the band, then converge all at once. The Apaches—and Clay—wouldn't stand a chance.

The attitude of the three scalp hunters changed when the mouth of a narrow canyon appeared and their companions had not. Goading their mounts, they tried to get ahead of the escapees and cut them off.

Clay understood their intent right away. Tucking the rifle to his shoulder, he took deliberate aim on the lead rider and fired. This time he wasn't quite so lucky as before: he missed the rider, but accidentally hit the man's horse.

Whoops burst from the Apaches when the scalp hunter and his mount tumbled, the animal to lie motionless, the scalp hunter to jump erect and scream curses at them.

Fiero shouted back, "That is how real men fight, you dogs!" Turning, he bent and exposed his backside. "And this is what I think of you, your mothers, and your fathers!"

The insult further enraged the man whose horse had been shot. He began firing madly, but the slugs all fell dozens of yards short, swirling puffs of dust into the air. When the rifle was empty, one of the others rode up and offered a hand so the shooter could swing up behind his saddle. Then the three men rode to the west.

The Apaches laughed, treating the episode as a fine joke. Clay didn't share in their mirth. It had delayed them, and any delay was costly if it gave Johnson the time he needed to catch up.

On reaching the canyon Clay felt more optimistic. The Chiricahuas were born and bred in mountains and could cover mountainous country on foot faster than white men could on horseback. He led them higher, stopping often to scan their back trail. To his delight, the scalp hunters did not show.

The course Clay had chosen brought them out of the canyon on its south rim. Here he had to decide whether to press on deeper into the mountains or to bear toward the northwest to the bluff. The matter was taken out of his hands when the sharp-eyed Amarillo gave a yell of warning.

A large group of riders was on the west rim, approaching rapidly. Seconds elapsed; then a second group materialized on the east rim.

Clay went higher, intentionally crossing boulder fields and going through thickets, instead of around. He used any trick that would give the horsemen grief, but his ruses proved unsuccessful. Slowly, but surely, the scalp hunters narrowed the distance.

On a switchback covered with pinon trees, Clay halted to rest. The scalp hunters were half a mile below, walking their mounts.

"We should hide and ambush them when they reach the top," Ponce proposed.

"The four of us against all of them?" Amarillo responded. "When they have a rifle for each man, and we have but one?"

Curious to know the exact odds, Clay moved a branch aside and counted their enemies. He was surprised to find a total of twenty-one since only seventeen scalp hunters had entered Sahuaripa and three had since been slain. Then he thought of the seven soldiers and got his total. Peering intently, he determined there were indeed two groups, a smaller bunch tailing a larger one by twenty or thirty yards.

Captain Rivera, apparently, was partial to the company he kept.

From the pinons the band climbed to a shelf boasting an odd mixture of ponderosa pines and prickly pear cactus. Clay stood deep in thought at the edge, frustrated because he was unable to come up with a brainstorm for saving their hides. He could have asked the Apaches for help, but his pride wouldn't let him. They were relying on him for the first time ever; he refused to let them down.

The west end of the shelf terminated in an almost sheer drop-off over a hundred yards from top to bottom. No one in his right mind would try to negotiate that steep a grade, yet when Clay discovered it, he smiled, aware it would be impossible for horses to handle.

"Follow me," Clay said and went over the side, without looking to see if the warriors did follow. The moment his soles hit the slope he began sliding uncontrollably. There was no way to stop. The best he could do was bend at the knees, keep his balance, and hope not to stumble.

A problem cropped up, though. The lower Clay went, the faster he went. Dirt and dust slewed out from under his feet, forming a choking cloud that obscured the Apaches.

Clay dug in his heels to slow his momentum, but he didn't slow one bit and only made the cloud worse. He twisted sideways, with the same result. Bending lower, he jammed the rifle stock into the ground, but the soil was so soft he couldn't get a purchase. Gradually, he gained more and more speed; the level land below rushed up to meet him incredibly quick.

Even though Clay was braced, he was in no wise prepared for the end of his long ride. His speed carried him a few yards across the flat tract, until friction slowed him enough for his soles to dig in. Unable to slide any further, yet with his body still moving at a brisk clip, he was thrown forward, as if shot from a cannon, to tumble end over end.

Clay thudded against a boulder and had the wind knocked out of him. Shoving onto an elbow, he saw the warriors strike bottom. Amazingly, they were able to stay upright by a clever method: on reaching the flatland, they began running just as soon as their feet touched down. In this way, their speed was swiftly spent.

"Tarnation. Why didn't I think of that?" Clay grumbled. Standing, he brushed himself off, then headed westward into the welcoming shelter of chaparral. Finding a hiding place, he lay low. His wait was short.

Blue Cap and company appeared on the shelf. Johnson could be seen gesturing angrily at the drop-off while walking back and forth. He tried to make several of his men go down, giving two of them rough shoves, but they were having none of it and flatly refused. Presently, the scalp hunters withdrew.

"Cowards!" Fiero said. "We have been running from cowards!"

"Cowards with guns are just as deadly as brave men with guns," Amarillo commented.

"They sound like words Delgadito would say," Clay mentioned, rising slowly. Thinking of his only friend in the world prompted Clay to head out. He noted the position of the sun, then trekked to the northwest, confident it would take the scalp hunters an hour or two to come the long way around, giving the Apaches and him plenty of time to reach their companions.

A rough hand abruptly fell on Clay's shoulder.

"I would talk with you, White Apache."

Clay slowed so Fiero could match his stride. "What about?"

"You saved us. Put your life in danger for us, for your enemies. Why?"

The truth would have angered the temperamental warrior, so Clay stretched it a mite by saying, "I do not think of you as my enemies. After all that has happened to us, I think of you as my friends."

"I would not have tried to save you."

"I know."

They hiked in silence for several minutes. Fiero glanced at Clay, his brow furrowed, then remarked, "I have never understood the white-eyes. You think wrong, live wrong, kill wrong. Until this day I have hated your kind as I have hated few others. Until this day I have never seen fit to call a white-eye friend."

"And now?"

"Now I think you have proven your words by your actions, which is the true measure of a man. You came into Sahuaripa knowing you might not leave again. You put yourself in danger for us. For me." Fiero paused. "I think I must think about this some more."

"Keep in mind," Clay said to help his cause, "I would do it again if I had to."

Fiero gave Clay the most peculiar look, grunted, and moved back to walk next to Ponce. The pair was soon speaking in low tones, gesturing now and again at Clay.

For Clay Taggart's part, he was elated at the turn of events. The Apaches, he believed, had finally begun to accept him. Even Fiero, whom Clay had once viewed as the most spiteful warrior alive. As a result, for the first time ever, Clay felt as if he were really and truly part of the band and not a despised outsider they accepted only because they had to.

Such musing occupied Clay for the next half an hour. They came to an *arroyo* and wound into it, walking on the shaded side. Clay was in the lead, rounding a bend, when he heard the nicker of a horse. Flattening against the wall, he motioned to the others as they appeared. Fiero melted into a crack, Ponce hid behind a bush, and Amarillo went prone.

The dull thump of hoofs confirmed they were not alone. A saddle creaked. Spurs jangled.

The rider was on the rim above, moving toward the mouth of the *arroyo*. His shadow flowed along the ground toward Clay, showing the man's posture, showing also the dark outline of the rifle he held.

Clay tilted his head back but couldn't see the man or the horse. He hoped the animal wouldn't catch their scent, or it was liable to give them away.

After the rider had gone by, Clay took a short step and glanced up. He did not need to see the man's face to know it was a scalp hunter, but he was at a loss to figure out how the cutthroat got there. Johnson's pack of bloodthirsty butchers was supposed to be somewhere to the southwest, not in front of the Apaches and him.

There could only be one explanation, Clay deduced. Someone, either one of Johnson's men or a soldier, had known of a short-cut. Somehow, the scalp hunters had gotten ahead and were now scouring the countryside in all directions in order to locate tracks. And the rider on the rim would shortly do just that. At the *arroyo* mouth he would see their footprints and give a signal.

Clay couldn't allow that to happen. Giving his rifle to Amarillo, he sprinted along the base of the wall until he was twenty feet below and behind the rider. He palmed his knife, gripping the smooth hilt firmly, and took on the fly a narrow game trail that led upward at an angle.

The scalp hunter heard steps and twisted at the selfsame second Clay cleared the top. Clay took a flying leap as the killer lifted the rifle, sailing clear over the mount's hind end. His hand smacked its rump, and the little extra push was enough to propel him into the rider.

The bearded, smelly badman rammed an arm into Clay's midsection in an attempt to unseat him, but Clay clung to the rider with one hand and shoved his knife into the man's abdomen.

Roaring like a stuck bear, the rider seized hold of Clay and deliberately threw himself from his animal. Whether he intended to plummet over the edge of the *arroyo* was another matter, but that is precisely what happened. Clay frantically shifted, trying to get on top so the scalp hunter would bear the brunt of the fall. In this he was only partially successful.

Piercing pangs shot through Clay on impact. It felt as if every rib on his right side had been shattered. He lost his grip on his knife, got both hands on the ground, and pushed erect.

The cutthroat, defying belief, was also rising, the bloody hilt jutting from his gut. He snarled at Clay as might a riled panther, gripped the knife, and yanked it out. A geyser of blood spewed forth, but the man was unaffected.

Clay Taggart ducked as his own blade was speared at his throat. He reached for his Colt, his arm a blur, remembering too late he had given both pistols away. The scalp hunter lunged, trying to slice open his stomach. Clay leaped backward, and in doing so, smacked into the *arroyo* wall. His hands touched it and came away with handfuls of dirt.

Sliding to the right, Clay let the man lunge again. Like striking rattlers, both of Clay's arms snaked upward. The dirt caught the hard case flush in the face, in the eyes, and he quickly retreated, blinking and wiping a forearm over them. Clay sprang, batting the knife aside with his left hand, even as his right fist slammed into the man's jaw.

The scalp hunter's legs buckled, and down he went. Clay was on him in a twinkling, wresting the knife loose, reversing his grip so he could streak the knife on high and then stab the killer, not once, but four times in swift succession. At the final stroke the man vented a gurgling groan and went limp.

Clay could never say what made him do that which he did next. A powerful compulsion came over him to lift the dead man's head by the hair and yip like an Apache. He also felt a fleeting urge to mutilate the scalp hunter, to gouge his knife into the killer's face until it was unrecognizable, but he controlled the impulse.

Exultant, Clay flung the head from him in contempt and turned to find the three Apaches regarding him with approval. Fiero—the same Fiero who had once passionately vowed to rub him out—grinned and complimented him.

"Well fought, White Apache!"

Amarillo brought over the rifle. "You must let us do some of the killing sometime. It is not good for a warrior to want to do it all himself."

"The next one is yours," Clay assured him. He spied the cutthroat's rifle lying in the dirt, picked it up, and threw it to Fiero. "This is yours to keep," he said, knowing full well the implications.

Among the Apaches, firearms were hard to come by. Each and every gun was cherished by its owner, kept clean at all times and protected from the elements. Because such a high value was placed on guns, particularly rifles, when a warrior gave one to another warrior it was looked upon as a mark of brotherhood. There was no higher honor.

So, on being told the Winchester was his, Fiero so forgot himself as to display outright astonishment. He looked at Clay, looked at the rifle, then at Clay again. "It is a fine gun. I am honored, White Apache."

For that all too brief interval there was an unspoken bond between the two men—one white and one red—a bond that had never existed before. It was an awkward interval, in which they stared at one another and said nothing. Then the bond was broken by an urgent whisper.

"White Apache, listen!" Amarillo said. "More horses come!"

Clay spun. Sure enough, hoofs drummed further down the *arroyo*. "Against the wall!" he commanded, thumbing back the hammer on his rifle. Each of them cocked his weapon, and they were ready when more shadows came to a halt almost at their very feet and a rough voice bellowed, "Lookee! There's Lester's horse!"

"Forget the damn horse! Look down there! It's Lester himself!"

Inhaling, Clay leaped into the open, pivoting as he did, and shouted, "Now!"

Three scalp hunters were above. Three men all of the same stripe. Grimy, grungy killers who satisfied their lust for blood by slaying a people they rated lower than human. In their estimation the only good Indian was a dead Indian, and they had made scores of good Indians in their time. But their time ended then and there.

Clay worked the lever in a frenzy, his Winchester blasting, blasting, blasting. On either side, the Apaches did the same. Pistols and rifles boomed and cracked.

The three scalp hunters never had a prayer. Bullet holes blossomed in their faces, in their necks, in their chests. One man lost both eyes. Another had his nose blown clean off. A third was shot through his open mouth. They were literally riddled.

"We must catch their horses!" Clay shouted as the bodies toppled. He dashed to the narrow trail and took it to the top again, but he was too late to catch a single animal. They had all raced off and were trotting toward a grassy stretch several hundred yards off. But the horse belonging to the first hard case, the man named Lester, had only gone fifty yards or so and was standing with its reins caught in scrub brush.

Clay jogged toward it and was passed by the three Apaches as if he was standing still. He stopped to reload while they caught the first horse and went after the others. In the time it took him to gather up the weapons of the slain scalp hunters, the Apaches had caught all four animals and returned, riding.

Fiero held out the reins to Lester's mount, a fine sorrel. "This is yours to keep," he said.

"I thank you," Clay said sincerely. The friendly gesture was Fiero's way of showing gratitude for the rifle. Little did the warrior know that Clay had just started to sway his opinion.

"And these are yours," Clay said, holding up a Remington revolver he had stripped from one of the bodies, along with a cartridge belt crammed with cartridges.

Once more Fiero betrayed his surprise. "I can never repay you for your kindness."

"Your friendship is all I want," Clay said. "From all of you." To demonstrate his point, he passed out rifles and pistols to Ponce and Amarillo and told the warriors to keep them.

"You are very generous," the latter commented.

"As are all *Shis-Inday* after a raid," Clay said, referring to the Apache practice of sharing the common spoils among the warriors who took part. Blankets, food, horses, and most other goods were evenly divided. But not guns. Rifles and pistols belonged to whoever claimed them on the field of battle, which made Clay's gifts unique.

Clay couldn't resist a chuckle. He flattered himself that Delgadito would be immensely proud of him when Delgadito learned how he had won the favor of the others. It was a ploy worthy of a true Apache, one Delgadito might have used.

Suddenly Ponce pointed and said, "Blue Cap!"

Fiero pointed too, only in an entirely different direction. "The *soldados* also!"

From the west came Ben Johnson, from the north Captain Rivera. Clay turned the sorrel southward and applied his heels. He had to continue to lead both parties away from the bluff, and the sole avenue of flight open led ever deeper into the mountains.

It felt strange to be on a saddle again. Clay could not seem to get comfortable. He disdained using the stirrups, preferring to ride as the Apaches did, his legs loose against the sorrel's sides.

A few rifle shots shattered the hot air, but none came close enough to be bothersome. Clay had his choice of a canyon and a mountain slope, and he choose the canyon.

He was counting on coming out the opposite side well ahead of the scalp hunters, maybe even with enough time to set up an ambush.

Everything was going so well that Clay wanted to pinch himself. The three warriors had been saved. They had horses and guns. Delgadito and Cuchillo Negro were safe. And soon he would turn the tables on Ben Johnson. So much had happened so fast he had a hard time believing it wasn't all a dream. His luck never ran this way.

Clay glanced over a shoulder to be sure they were maintaining their lead. The scalp hunters and soldiers hadn't gained a yard. Rather, they were pacing themselves, holding their mounts to a brisk trot, perhaps so their horses would have strength left for a short spurt later on.

Let the no-account polecats try! Clay reflected. A newfound confidence fired him with vigor; he couldn't wait to put his trap into effect. He could just imagine the look on Delgadito's face if they returned bearing Johnson's scalp! Delgadito would be so grateful, Clay figured, that the warrior would do anything for him.

The mouth of the canyon was wide but the walls narrowed the farther the band went. Clay wasn't worried. Canyons were often wider at the ends than in the middle. He checked for offshoots, for side canyons where they could hide and fire from when their pursuers caught up, but there were none. The walls were solid, high, and sheer, too sheer to be scaled on foot, even if there had been a trail.

Amarillo came alongside Clay and hefted the rifle Clay had given him. "I have misjudged you, Lickoyee-shis-inday. I wanted you to know that."

"We all make mistakes."

"If you are ever in need, you only have to ask. Or if you are ever caught by our enemies, know that I will do what I can to free you."

"We should all help one another. It is the only way we can survive."

"I know you have wanted us to aid you in your fight against the white-eye who wronged you. And I admit I did not want to lift a finger on your behalf, before now."

"You will not regret your decision. There will be much plunder, many horses and guns."

"And what else matters in life, eh?" Amarillo said, smiling.

Once Clay would have listed five or six other things: a good woman, children, money, land, his health. Now he grinned and responded, "Nothing that I can see."

The canyon angled to the east. Clay took the turn at a gallop and saw another bend ahead, which was good. The scalp hunters would slow down so as not to be bushwhacked, and would fall farther behind. Just as Clay wanted.

Brimming with self-assurance, Clay negotiated the next bend and instantly reined up in consternation. His plan had gone terribly awry. Twenty yards in front of him was a rock wall. The canyon had turned out to be a box canyon. Instead of leading the scalp hunters into a trap, he had trapped himself and the Apaches.

Unless Clay thought of something, they were as good as dead.

Chapter Twelve

The man known as the White Apache stared in baffled anger at the impassable barrier, then wheeled his sorrel. He fed a round into the chamber of his rifle as the warriors clustered around him.

"What do we do now?" Ponce asked.

"They can keep us pinned down in here and starve us out," Fiero said.

"Or they can go around to the top and pick us off from up there," Amarillo noted.

Clay held the Winchester close to his side. "They will do none of those things."

"Why not?" Ponce demanded.

"Because we will not be here. We are going to charge them."

"They outnumber us," the young warrior said. "They have many more guns."

"We will have surprise on our side," Clay countered.

"That is not enough," Ponce stubbornly persisted.

159

"Then stay here and die." Clay rode close to the bend and listened to the approaching thunder. It would be a minute or two yet, he figured, and was surprised that he felt no fear since he did not count on making it out alive. He gazed at the Apaches; then, at the heights above. Of all the places in which to die, this was the very last place he would have expected. Of all the circumstances under which he could have passed on, these were circumstances he would never have predicted, not in a million years.

Life was downright peculiar at times, Clay reflected. A man never knew from one day to the next what tomorrow would bring. Joy. Sorrow. Love. Betrayal. They were all rolls of the dice, luck or bad luck, as the case might be. And since a man couldn't predict his fate, couldn't guarantee his happiness no matter how hard he tried, it was wisest to take what came along without complaint and make the best of it.

Clay made himself a promise. If, by some miracle, he did survive, he was going to make the most of every minute of life remaining to him. No more regrets. No more wishful thinking. He would take each day one at a time, and the Devil be hanged!

Voices sounded past the bend. Clay looked at the warriors and grinned. "Let's show these buzzards how men die," he said in English. When they stared at him quizzically, he declared in their own tongue, "Kill as many of the dogs as you can!"

Then, lashing his reins, Clay galloped around the bend, the Winchester tucked to his shoulder. He had timed the attempt just right. The scalp hunters and soldiers were in the straight stretch between the two bends, bunched together but not so tightly a rider couldn't barrel through them.

In the forefront rode Ben Johnson, wearing the Union

cap he had worn the day he deserted from the army. Clay took a hasty bead and fired, but the alert renegade swerved and took a flying leap, landing behind a boulder.

A chorus of savage whoops erupted behind Clay as he aimed at another target and fired. Three more rifles cracked. The volley slew the front rank of scalp hunters, toppling men right and left. The rest, bewildered by the unexpected attack, tried to turn their mounts and flee or take cover, instead of shooting back. Confusion reigned, confusion that enabled Clay and the Apaches to plow through the hard cases with misleading ease.

The *soldados* were another matter. Trailing the scalp hunters by a dozen yards, they had more time to react, to gird themselves, to level their rifles.

Captain Rivera filled Clay's sights, and although Clay had no wish to kill a man who had never done anything to him, who was only doing his job, Clay squeezed the trigger. Rivera sailed backwards as Clay closed on the enlisted men. The Apaches were hot on his heels, and between them, they dispensed death on all sides. Fighting at close quarters, using guns and knives, the warriors carved a path through the *soldados* that left five of the six Mexicans thrashing on the ground in the convulsions preceding death.

The second bend beckoned. Clay rode faster, taking the bend a few heartbeats before a ragged series of shots showed that the scalp hunters had recovered and were out for blood. He glanced back, saw all the Apaches were unharmed. Fiero yipped so Clay responded in kind.

Like a pack of wolves celebrating a kill, the Apaches sped down the canyon to its mouth. Clay reined up so abruptly the sorrel had to dig in its hoofs and slide to a stop. He surveyed boulders on both sides of the opening, then nodded. "We end it here."

The Apaches, who had halted the moment he had, looked at one another.

"We can escape," Ponce said.

"They cannot stop us," Amarillo added.

Clay commenced replacing the spent rounds in his rifle. "Go if you want. No one will hold it against you. But you know and I know that Blue Cap will never rest until he has taken revenge on us. He will hunt us wherever we go, north or south of the border."

"White Apache is right," Fiero stated.

"The only way to put an end to this, once and for all time, is to end it here and now," Clay went on. "There is only one way out of the canyon. They will have to go past us."

"They still outnumber us," Amarillo said.

"Who is counting?" Clay replied. He rode to the right, concealed the sorrel behind a boulder the size of a cabin, and took up a position in the small boulders closer to the mouth. Fiero joined him. Ponce and Amarillo hid across the way.

"We must not let one go by," Clay said. "If word should get out, the state of Sonora will put so high a bounty on our heads that every scalp hunter in Mexico and every greedy Indian hater up north will be after our hair."

Fiero levered a round into his rifle. "To the death," he said grimly. "I would not have it any other way."

Clay hunkered down. He recollected the first time he had set eyes on Ben Johnson, during the raid on Delgadito's encampment, and the horrible images of women and children being mercilessly slaughtered seared into his brain. Women, split from crown to chin by sabers or shot so full of holes they resembled sieves. Children, crushed under the driving hoofs of horses or run down for sport and impaled on knives. And here he was avenging them, a white man avenging people who had been complete strangers to him. Yet, in an odd sort of way, it felt right to be there, to be able to make the scalp hunters pay for their years of slaughtering innocents.

A bee buzzed past. Clay squinted up at the sun, wondering why Johnson was taking so long. Probably the cutthroats were tending to their wounded, he reasoned, or figuring out what to do next.

"They come," Fiero declared.

A few seconds later Clay heard them too. He rested the barrel of his rifle on the boulder in front of him and lowered his cheek to the stock. The scalp hunters would be there soon. His thumb curled back the hammer, and he lightly touched his finger to the trigger.

"Blue Cap is mine," Fiero said.

Before Clay could respond, riders appeared up the canyon. Four abreast, and they were flying like the wind, as if they knew their lives depended on it. Dragged behind their mounts were bundles of brush that raised great clouds of dust, so much dust that those behind the first four were completely obscured.

"Damn!" Clay snapped, realizing he had been outfoxed. Johnson had anticipated the ambush; under the cover of the dust most of the scalp hunters hoped to get away.

Fiero opened up. Clay joined him at the same instant Ponce and Amarillo did. Three of the killers were hit, but only two fell. The wounded man clung to his saddle, bent low over his animal's neck. None of the horses slowed in the slightest.

Clay fired twice into the huge dust cloud even though

he knew he was wasting ammunition. Vague shapes were all he could see of the scalp hunters. Getting a bead on one was impossible.

Rising, Clay ran to the sorrel and vaulted into the saddle. He had to stop the scalp hunters one way or the other. Feeding a new round into the chamber of his rifle, he galloped past the boulder.

Already the cutthroats had swept past the canyon mouth and were fleeing northward. The riderless mounts had veered to either side of the main body, reducing the amount of dust. Some of the scalp hunters bringing up the rear were now visible.

Clay banged off two shots, saw two hard cases drop. Then he concentrated on overtaking the main bunch. Among them would be Ben Johnson, the man Clay wanted the most.

A glance showed the Apaches were following, but they were sixty or seventy yards behind and would be unable to overtake Clay before he overtook Johnson.

As if on signal the scalp hunters scattered, separating into twos and threes and making off in all different directions. Anxiously Clay scanned them. A speeding pair to the northwest caught his attention. One of the riders wore a telltale blue cap.

Clay gave the sorrel its head. He saw Johnson look, saw the sneer that slashed the butcher's face. In defiance Clay yipped, then settled down to the job at hand.

Scalp hunters were skilled horsemen. The violent life they had chosen honed their skill. Traveling long distances as they did, often days or weeks at a stretch, over the most rugged of terrain in order to strike at an Apache encampment they had received word of, these men could hold their own against anyone, anywhere.

So Clay wasn't upset at being unable to catch the pair

right away. He was content merely to keep them in sight, and for the next three-quarters of an hour that is exactly what he did. He neither gained nor lost any ground.

Suddenly the two badmen vanished, sinking from sight as if swallowed by the earth. Clay knew better. They had gone into a gully or a wash and might be waiting for him to show himself so they could shoot him to ribbons.

Clay was too smart for that. He slanted to the west and slowed, the Winchester cocked and held at shoulder height. In a bit he spied the gully, which crossed his path from east to west. Slowing even more, to a walk, Clay stood in the stirrups for a glimpse of the bottom. But the gully was too deep.

Cautiously, Clay approached the rim. When he was fifteen feet away, he climbed down and advanced on tip toe. Crouching at the edge, he scoured the bottom and saw only brush. There were no scalp hunters, no hoofprints, indicating to Clay that the pair had gone eastward.

Climbing back on the sorrel, Clay rode into the gully and up the other side. From his new vantage point he could see a little farther than before, but it proved unnecessary. For no sooner had he gained the top than Johnson and the other scalp hunter burst from the gully hundreds of feet distant and galloped to the southeast, toward Sahuaripa.

"No you don't," Clay said under his breath as he gave chase. He would ride the sorrel into the ground, if need be, to stop them from reaching safety. And he just might have to do that. The sorrel was flecked with sweat and showing signs of being tired. A few more miles and it would be too tuckered out to stand, let alone gallop.

Clay persisted anyway. The stakes were too high for him to quit. Countless lives would be lost, women and

children slaughtered piteously, their remains left to rot
or to serve as food for buzzards.

Another hour went by. The sorrel flagged but gamely
responded to Clay's goading. Thankfully, Johnson and
the other man also slowed, so Clay was able to stay
almost within rifle range. Presently, there appeared a
knobby spine of land that, ages ago, must have been a
mountain chain, which had long since been worn down
by wind and rain. Boulders dotted the spine, affording
ample spots to take cover, which is what Johnson and
his companion did. They disappeared into a wide notch
between two boulders.

Clay swung wide, suspecting another trick. They
might know the area, he speculated, might be able
to work their way over the spine without being seen.
Consequently, he rode all the way around and reined
up in the shade of a mammoth slab of rock. From here
Clay would be able to see if the scalp hunters made a
break for Sahuaripa.

Taking the Winchester, Clay climbed onto a tear
shaped boulder, covered his eyes with his hand, and
scoured the spine. Somewhere in that maze was Ben
Johnson, but finding him would be like finding a needle
in a haystack. Clay could spend days wandering among
those boulders without accomplishing a thing.

Maybe, Clay reflected, Johnson was counting on Clay
to give up in time. If Johnson knew where to find water,
the scalp hunter could wait Clay out. Clay somehow
had to flush the two killers into the open or locate their
hiding place.

Near the middle of the ancient spine reared a towering
column of stone that looked as if a giant had taken a lot
of great flat boulders and piled them one on top of the
other. From there, Clay figured, he might be able to

spot Johnson. The problem was reaching it and scaling it without being shot.

Sliding down, Clay led the sorrel eastward by the reins. From cover to cover he crept, ever nearer the column. When the sorrel lifted its head and pricked its ears, he halted, listening with bated breath. Whatever the horse heard, he didn't. In a minute the animal lost interest, its head drooping, so he went on.

In the shadow of the column, Clay ground-hitched the sorrel. He stepped to the base of the imposing natural wonder, hooked his fingertips on the lip of a boulder above him, and, muscles bulging, pulled himself high enough to get a purchase for his feet. The climb, he discovered, would be extremely difficult. He paused, pondering his next move.

It was then that someone coughed.

Clay was off the column, crouched at its base, before the cough died. The sorrel was gazing to the southwest so he went in that direction, hugging the bottoms of the boulders, placing each foot down lightly in order not to make any noise. A man like Ben Johnson would have the senses of a cat. Taking him by surprise would be hard to do.

A hint of moisture in the air gave the cutthroats away, a trace of coolness that Clay could practically taste. Water was nearby, and where there was water, there would be the scalp hunters.

Clay dropped to his hands and knees and crawled. He had covered only a few yards when softly spoken words reached his ears.

"—don't much like this sittin' and doin' nothin'."

"We stay put until nightfall, Simms. Quit your bellyaching."

"We can outrun him, I tell you. His horse has to be

as tired as ours, Ben. We can beat him to town."

"Maybe so. But I'm not taking any chances. You've fought enough Apaches to know not to take them for granted. There might be more between here and Sahuaripa."

"I'm willing to try."

"I'm not."

While the scalp hunters talked, Clay moved closer. A single boulder was all that blocked them from his view. He could see their horses over to his left, heads hanging as the animals dozed. To his right lay a small spring, its surface as smooth as glass. The killers, Clay guessed, were sitting with their backs to the boulder.

That gave Clay an idea. Setting the rifle quietly down, he rose, wincing when his knee popped. There was no reaction by Johnson or Simms, so he reached up, caught hold, and climbed.

"I've never seen you so spooked by one Injun before," Simms said. "What's so special about this son of a bitch that we couldn't make a stand?"

"He's different."

"How different?"

"I can't put my finger on it, but there's something about him. He doesn't look right."

"If anyone else told me such nonsense, I'd think the sun had baked his brain."

Clay was halfway up the boulder, clinging with fingers and toes like an oversized lizard. Grains of dirt fell from under his left hand, and he feared the scalp hunters would hear but they continued whispering.

"Didn't you see his face? His build?" Johnson demanded gruffly. "He's either a breed or a white man."

"The Apaches ride with a white-eye?" Simms chuckled. "Never happen, boss. They hate every last mother's son of us. They'd sooner skin us alive."

"He looked white, damn it."

"Whatever you say."

The next moment, Clay gained the flat top of the boulder and paused to catch his breath. Below him were two hats, the Union cap and a black, filthy Stetson.

Ben Johnson shifted. "I want you to take your slicker and make sure we erased all our tracks between here and where the boulders began."

"There's no need. We were real careful. We didn't miss one."

"Do it anyway," Johnson growled.

Muttering under his breath, the man named Simms rose. "All right, all right. Don't get your dander up." He took a step toward the horses, then stopped to stretch, turning toward the boulder as he did. "Just when I was hankering for a na—"

Clay saw the hard case's eyes lock on him and launched himself into the air, his knife clutched in his right hand. It would have been simpler to use his pistols, simpler to shoot both men dead before they even knew he was there, but that would have been too painless an end for men who had caused so much suffering, who reveled in slaughter and bloodshed. Clay wanted to do to them as they had done to so many others. He wanted to give them a taste of their own medicine. So he relied on the knife instead.

Simms opened his mouth wide to blurt a warning but Clay was on him sooner, his foot smashing into Simms's chest and propelling the stocky man backward into the horses. The animals naturally whinnied and shied away, one of them lashing out with its rear legs. A hoof thudded against Simms's head and he sprawled forward, either dazed or dead.

All this Clay glimpsed as he alighted and spun to face the most feared scalp hunter of all. Ben Johnson was rising, his hand stabbing for his six-shooter. Clay thrust, his knife nicking Johnson's arm as Johnson dodged to one side. The Colt slipped from the killer's fumbling grasp. Pressing his attack, Clay swung again and again, trying to gut his foe. Ben Johnson evaded the blows, then suddenly bent and whipped his own knife from a boot.

"Now try me, bastard!"

"Glad to," Clay responded.

Johnson blinked, grinning savagely. "I knew you were white! Damn your bones!"

Clay leaped and slashed. His blow was parried. Johnson skipped to the left. A gleaming blade rushed at Clay's head and would have split him like a melon had he not jerked his head back. Clay tried to ram his knife into the scalp hunter's gut, but the experienced Johnson glided aside.

They circled one another, each seeking an opening, their knives weaving small circles in the air. Johnson wore a determined look. There was no fear on his face. He had done this before, no doubt many times, and had always won. He was confident he would win again.

Clay tried a low cut, a high cut. Johnson backed up, or attempted to, but there was nowhere for him to go because he had unwittingly placed his back to the spring. His left foot slipped into the water, and he started to lose his balance.

Like a pouncing jaguar, Clay struck, jumping and stabbing, his knife sinking into Johnson's shoulder. He had aimed for the heart but Johnson twisted at the last moment. Their bodies collided, and they fell.

Water as frigid as ice closed around Clay Taggart. He sank under the surface, felt firm footing under him, and went to shove upward just as a heavy body hurtled into his torso and steely fingers found his throat. Ben Johnson had lost his knife but was no less deadly. Clay drove his blade at the scalp hunter's ribs and found his wrist gripped by a vise.

Grappling mightily, they tossed this way and that, Clay striving to break the grip on his neck and arm while Johnson strove to strangle him. Since Clay had not taken a deep breath before going under, there was precious little air in his lungs. Whether from strangulation or drowning, his end was assured, unless he could break free.

Johnson was smirking. He held fast, preventing Clay from reaching the surface. Blood seeped from the killer's wound, turning the water reddish.

No! Clay's mind screamed. It couldn't end this way! Dark spots danced before his eyes. He was weakening rapidly, his lungs on fire. In another few seconds his mouth would open and water would rush in, and that would be his finish. In desperation, he drove his knee into Johnson's groin. The grip on his wrist slackened, just enough for him to wrench his arm loose and spear the knife where he had planted his knee. He felt the blade sink into yielding flesh and saw Johnson's face reflect utter agony. Again Clay stabbed, and this time the scalp hunter released his neck and shot upward.

So did Clay. He gulped in air as he broke the surface and turned to discover Johnson was trying to scramble out. Two strokes brought Clay to the killer. Johnson, sensing his presence, whirled, and Clay sank his knife to the hilt into the man's chest. Ben Johnson uttered a gasp, went rigid, and collapsed.

Clay did some gasping of his own as he wedged both elbows on solid ground and heaved out of the pool. His first thought was of Simms, but when he looked, he saw both the stocky scalp hunter and one of the horses were gone. The man must have been afraid there were more Apaches and fled for his life.

Sucking in air, Clay sat up and stared at the body now floating with arms outstretched. It was over, finally, gratefully, over. He would rest a spell, then go find the Apaches and take them to Delgadito. Within two weeks they would be back in the States.

Miles and Lilly Gillett had better watch out.

Epilogue

Update to all Commands from Headquarters,
Fifth Cavalry

As a result of facts brought to light by the marshal of Tucson and the government of Mexico, the Adjutant-general's office has deemed it prudent to relay certain crucial information concerning the reputed White Apache.

It can now be confirmed that a band of renegade Apaches include a white man among their number. As incredible as this is to accept, Marshal Tom Crane and a highly respected rancher, Mr. Miles Gillett, have given sworn testimonies to this effect. The Mexican government has provided supporting evidence.

In light of these developments, this headquarters is coordinating an effort with civilian authorities to track down and capture the White Apache, who has been identified as Arizonan Clay Taggart. In the interim, should any law officer at the town, county, state or federal level apprehend him, they have been advised to transfer him to military custody.

Pertinent personal information concerning the White Apache is as follows:

TRUE NAME: Clayton Stonewall Taggart

AGE: 24

HEIGHT: 6′2″   WEIGHT: Estimated to be 190.

HAIR: Black   EYES: Blue

IDENTIFYING MARKS: According to Taggart's physician in Tucson, he has a two-inch scar on his left calf caused during a mishap involving a plow when he was only ten.

BACKGROUND: Until recently Taggart was a law-abiding rancher. For reasons that have yet to be established, he is believed to have tried to force himself on the wife of a neighbor and then killed one of the neighbor's punchers who tried to intervene. A posse tracked him to the Dragoons where they lost his trail. It was assumed he had met his death at the hands of Apaches until he appeared about a month ago and tried to abduct the neighbor's wife. (See Attachment #1.)

Just two days ago, this office received a report from Sonora concerning a raid by Apaches on the town of Sahuaripa. (See Attachment #2.) An American citizen in the employ of the Sonoran government, one Rufus Simms, has reported that a white man was with the war party.

As a result of the foregoing, this headquarters hereby directs all commands to step up their efforts to learn the whereabouts of this White Apache and to relay to this office any information that might assist in his capture or extermination.

Make no mistake. Headquarters wants this man, alive if at all possible, so he can stand trial for his actions, but if circumstances do not warrant this action, then he is to be slain on the spot.

Further updates will be released as they are required.

CHEYENNE

JUDD COLE

Born Indian, raised white, he swore he'd die a free man. Follow the adventures of Touch the Sky, as he searches for a world he can call his own!

#7: Comancheros. When a notorious Spanish slave trader captures their women and children, Touch the Sky and his brother warriors race to save them. It is a battle against time, and if the Cheyenne are too late, the glorious promise of their past will fade into a bleak and hopeless future.

___3496-4 $3.50 US/$4.50 CAN

#8: Flood Fury. Raised among frontier settlers, Touch the Sky returned to his tribe determined to lead them to their greatest victory. And he'd need all the trickery and daring he could muster when an old foe devised a diabolical plot to crush the Cheyennes' dreams of a glorious future.

___3546-4 $3.50 US/$4.50 CAN